DIARY OF A WITNESS

DIARY OF A WITNESS

CATHERINE RYAN HYDE

Alfred A. Knopf
New York

Thanks, as always, to Vance and Suzanne for being my trusted (and honest) "first readers." Special thanks to Diane Stevens, whose feedback helped shape the early trajectory of Ernie and Will's story. And a very special thanks to my friend Jenny for teaching me how to fish.

THIS IS A BORZOI BOOK PUBLISHED BY ALFRED A. KNOPF

Visit us on the Web! www.randomhouse.com/teens

Educators and librarians, for a variety of teaching tools, visit us at
www.randomhouse.com/teachers

Library of Congress Cataloging-in-Publication Data
Hyde, Catherine Ryan.
Diary of a witness/Catherine Ryan Hyde. — 1st ed.
p. cm.
Summary: Ernie, an overweight high school student and long-time target of bullies, relies on his best friend Will to watch his back until Will, overwhelmed by problems at home and guilt over his brother's death, seeks a final solution.
ISBN 978-0-375-85684-6 (trade) — ISBN 978-0-375-95684-3 (lib. bdg.) —
ISBN 978-0-375-85358-6 (e-book)
[1. Bullies — Fiction. 2. Obesity — Fiction. 3. High schools — Fiction. 4. Schools — Fiction.
5. Single-parent families — Fiction. 6. Emotional problems — Fiction. 7. Diaries — Fiction.]
I. Title.
PZ7.H96759Did 2009
[Fic] — dc22
2008040883

The text of this book is set in 12-point Goudy.

Printed in the United States of America
August 2009
10 9 8 7 6 5 4 3 2 1

First Edition

Random House Children's Books supports the First Amendment and celebrates the right to read.

In memory of Lenny Horowitz,
my high school English teacher.
One caring person can turn the tide.
And you did.

November 4th

Will Manson stood up for me today. Against the jocks. Stupid. Nice, but stupid. I wish he wouldn't do stuff like that. It's so wrong. Will's my best friend, though.

Oh, who am I kidding? He's my only friend.

It was gym class, which has got to be the worst of an already bad situation. But I'm pretty used to it. More or less. As much as you get used to a thing like that. I'd just gotten out of the shower, and I was walking back to my corner to get dressed. As fast as I safely could. It doesn't pay to go too fast. It draws them. Like when dogs see a cat running away. It brings out the worst in them.

I got snapped with a towel from behind. Right on the

butt. It hurt, but I kept that to myself. It almost knocked off the towel I was wearing, but I grabbed it and held tight. Laughter from the rear, then some comments about laying off the Ho Hos and Twinkies. Nothing I don't hear pretty much every day of my life.

Then I heard Will's voice. He said, "Why don't you leave him alone?"

Really stupid. I was almost to my corner. Then it would have been over anyway. All he was doing was pouring Zippo lighter fluid on the fire. Still, you have to like him for stuff like that. In a weird sort of way.

By the time I looked around, the jocks had him by the throat with his back up against the wall. The usual suspects. There were five of them. I'm not even sure I know all their names. I'm pretty sure there's a Mike and a Dave in there somewhere. Then again, you can't throw a rock into a group of guys without hitting a Mike or a Dave. And you know what? They're cowards. Know how I know? Because they always attack in a pack, like a bunch of coyotes. Only cowards would be sure to outnumber their helpless victim by five to one.

Will isn't fat. But he catches it all the same. I think it's partly being new. Also smart doesn't help. Plus usually when he opens his mouth, something geeky will fall out. He's skinny, too skinny, and has big ears that stick out away from his head. And the worst acne ever. Sometimes it hurts to look at him. But I do anyway. I'm no picnic, either, so I still do. I think if his skin cleared up and he got his ears pinned by a plastic surgeon, he might be okay. If he never once talked.

The chief coward was talking so close to Will's face that you could see Will blink because he was getting spit on. "And what'll you do if we don't, huh, Charlie? Tell your mother? Oh, that's right. You don't *have* one."

I'll say this for Will. He didn't go at them. I could see how easy it would have been. I could see it on his face. I was thinking, Fight the urge. Be calm. I mean, what good does it do to charge five big jocks? They could just beat you to a pulp and walk away laughing.

I watched Will's face, and it just got redder and redder.

Will moved here from L.A. with his father at the beginning of the school year because his mother left them for some guy. We hit it off right away, because we have three big things in common. We each only have one parent. We each really like to fish. Even though his fishing and my fishing are pretty different things. And, most important, neither one of us has even one other person who wants to be our friend.

He doesn't talk much about his mother. The one time it came up, he just said what he always says about home: "That's life in the Manson family." Will thinks he was shot down before he was even born, because it's so hard to grow up with the name of a famous murderer. I think maybe he's being too dramatic. But I'm not sure he's entirely wrong. He takes a lot of crap for it. That's why they call him Charlie. That should be the worst thing they ever call us.

But you'd think they'd leave you alone about a thing like your mother. I mean, *your mother*. Damn. Something's got to be sacred. Instead they attack you on just that front. Like they have to call you a space alien for having that happen to you. Otherwise a thing like that could happen to them, too.

It's a theory, anyway. I'm full of theories about the popular guys. I'll never know if I'm right, though, because I'll never be one of them.

Poor Will. I never saw anybody get that red. The guy who was holding him called him Lobster Boy, and they all walked away laughing.

I got dressed fast, and Will and I walked out into the hall together. I always breathe when I get out into the hall. Like I'm breathing for the first time ever. Not that I haven't been tortured in the hall, but gym is worse.

I said, "Why do you do stuff like that, Will?"

He said, "You're welcome."

"Yeah, okay. It's nice and all. But it just makes it worse." The trick is to get small. Never look in their eyes. Never look at them at all. Just look down at the ground and try to get so small you're hardly even there. That's the only thing that helps. Except when it doesn't.

"You're right," he said. "You raise an interesting point,

young Ernie." That was a line we heard in a TV movie. We've been using it ever since. "If I really wanted to help you, I'd figure a way to get you out of gym altogether. And I might have just the thing."

"I'm not going to maim myself. If that's what you mean."

While we walked, I did the usual routine where I found lots of reasons to turn my head. If we passed a locker with stickers on it, I turned to read them. If a pretty girl walked by the other way, I followed her with my eyes until my head was almost all the way around. Pure ruse. Not that I don't like pretty girls, but it's not in me to stare. I was watching our backs. Making sure nobody was bearing down from the rear. But you can't just keep glancing nervously over your shoulder. Not unless you have a death wish. That's like the equivalent of bleeding into the water if you're a fish. You become this living, breathing advertisement for sharks.

"I knew a guy in L.A. who got a pass from gym. All he had to do was tell the guidance counselor a heartfelt story of grief."

"He just told him he was suffering in there?" Nothing is that easy. Right?

"No, he told him he was gay."

"I'm not gay."

"Neither was this guy. But he said he was. And that he was so scared because he thought every time he cut his eyes away, the other boys would know. Very sad story."

"They didn't make him go to counseling or anything?"

"No way, Jose. They can't do that. It's discrimination. He wasn't mentally ill. He was gay. Be proud, Ernie. You are a proud, well-adjusted young gay man. You just can't hack dressing with the boys. They'll pretend to understand, but really they're so paranoid they don't want you dressing with the other boys, either."

"Wow. I don't know." My brain was spinning around. How come when something really hurts, the only solutions hurt just as bad? "I'm not sure which is worse. Gym class or telling the guidance counselor I'm gay."

"Tough choices. Indeed." Will talks like that. Actually says things like indeed. "But consider this. Gym class is every day. You only have to tell this story once."

He had a point there. "I'll sleep on it," I said.

"Get Mrs. Menendez. She's sympathetic. Besides, I have a lot in common with Mrs. Menendez."

"Name one thing."

Will rolled his eyes at me. Sometimes he just couldn't believe I was so stupid. His idea of stupid was anybody who couldn't follow his twisted train of thought. "Alex, I'll take Famous Murderers for five hundred. Answer: the Menendez brothers. Question: Who are the two affluent young men who murdered their parents in cold blood with a shotgun?"

I shook my head. "You have murderers on the brain."

"Alas," he said. That's another thing he actually said. Alas. "My legacy."

Then we made a sharp right into biology lab. Without incident. We actually made it from the gym to the biology lab without incident. Red-letter day.

Now I seriously have to sleep on this Mrs. Menendez thing. That's got to be a weird thing to sleep on. I can just see myself tossing and turning a lot tonight.

Mrs. Menendez sat back in her chair and sighed. Her fingers were in that steeple mode. I wonder why people do that. They act like it helps them think or something. Like their brain is in their fingers.

"I understand this is a very tough issue for you, Ernie." I got the sense that this whole thing involved practice. The serious look of pity. The understanding. Like an actor who can do a part without even much thinking. "But I really hate to see you miss out on physical education entirely. P.E. is so important."

"Especially for me, right?"

She shot me a hurt look. I bet she practiced that, too. "Now, Ernie, you know I didn't say that."

No, but you were thinking it. But I didn't say that. I just stuck with the no. I just said, "No. You didn't." But you were thinking it.

"Maybe we can work something else out."

"Like what?" This was already taking a bad turn. She should be writing out my pass by now.

"Maybe Mr. Bayliss will let you use the gym during lunch hour, or after school. Tell you what. I'll write him a note, and you take it to him right now. And then the two of you can talk about what to do."

"I don't want Mr. Bayliss to know about this!"

"Well, how can we excuse you from P.E. without telling him? Let him help you, Ernie. You have to be willing to let people help you."

Why did I let Will talk me into this? I should've known this would turn into a major disaster. See, this is the problem with small-town living. You keep running into people who actually care. It's so irritating.

While I was feeling sorry for myself, she was writing out the note.

"Thanks," I said, and stuck it in my jacket pocket. Where I knew it would stay. Maybe forever. Or maybe when I got home I would burn it.

I showed up to gym class fifth period as usual. I knew I was in deep doo-doo when I heard Mr. Bayliss say, "Ernie Boyd? Anybody seen Ernie Boyd?" I was thinking about running away. Skipping entirely. Maybe even leaving school. Then I saw his head sticking around the corner. He had this really thick sandy hair that was cut so short it stuck straight up on top. It made him look like a scrub brush, only upside down. "Ah, there you are, Ernie. You have some kind of note you were supposed to show me?"

I could hear my heart pounding. I knew the panic on my face would give me away. "Uh. No."

He cocked his head over to one side. "No? Mrs. Menendez said she wrote you a note to bring me."

"Oh. *That* note. Yes."

"You still have it?"

"Uh. No."

"Well then, how about if I call her and get her down here for a little conference?"

"Uh. No. You know what? I think I *do* remember where I put that note."

"My office," he said. And then the scrub brush disappeared.

Mr. Bayliss had shelves full of trophies lining the walls of his office. Must have been from sports teams in the old days. All this year's sports teams bite.

I just sat there feeling about an inch tall while he read the note. I also felt kind of sick to my stomach. But maybe that was a good thing. Maybe if I threw up in his office, he'd forget all about the note. But it wasn't really bad enough. It wouldn't turn into throwing up, but it wouldn't go away.

He set down the note and looked right at me. I looked at my shoes.

"Ernie," he said. It wasn't good the way he said it. "You're not gay."

"You don't know that. How can you know what's inside of me?"

"Ernie, Ernie, Ernie. Just last week I heard you talking about Amy McPhee and how hot she is. The week before that, you came in here with a Victoria's Secret catalog in your gym bag."

How humiliating. "I didn't know you saw that." That was a bad answer. I should have said I was in denial, or putting up a brave front. This was just getting worse and worse. I would've given anything to start this morning all over.

"I know why you want to get out of gym class," he said. "It's no more embarrassing than being gay. I would think you'd've told the truth. The truth is no harder."

"Oh yes, sir. Yes it is, too. The truth is always harder. Because it's the truth."

Mr. Bayliss sat back and sighed. And put his fingers in that steeple mode. I kid you not. They must all rehearse together. They must cover this stuff in teacher school. "Make you a deal," he said.

I had a feeling I wasn't going to like this deal.

He pointed to the shower in the corner of his office. His own private shower. "See that shower? That's your shower for the rest of the year. And this is your dressing room."

I couldn't believe it. I didn't hate the deal. He was helping me. They never actually help you. It was amazing. "Cool. Thanks."

"Here's what you have to do for me, though."

Oh. Should've known. That was way too good to be true.

He pointed to the full-length mirror across from the shower. "See that mirror?"

"Yeah . . ." Did he think I was blind or something?

"And that scale next to it?"

Uh-oh. This was getting ugly. The scale was one of those vicious doctor's office things with the weights that slide over, so you see the answer right in front of your nose. "Okay. What about it?"

"When you get out of the shower, I want you to stand in front of that mirror and look at yourself. And then get on the scale."

I could feel myself getting dizzy. My heart was pounding in my ears, and it was like all these silent voices were screaming at me to get away. Just start running and never stop. Like I could really do that even if I tried. I don't think I said anything at all.

"Look, I'm not trying to shame you," he said. "That's why I'm giving you your privacy. I don't want you to be ridiculed. And I'm not saying you should ridicule yourself. I just want you to keep your eyes open. Look the problem head-on. I don't want to help you be in denial about it."

I just kept looking at my shoes.

I never look in full-length mirrors. Never. If I catch a glimpse of myself in a store window, I quick look away again. We don't even have full-length mirrors at our house. My mother doesn't want them, and neither do I.

"Ernie. Do we have a deal?"

"Yes, sir." It was better than showering and dressing with the other guys. Besides, if I didn't look, and I didn't weigh, he would never know.

"Okay, good. I'll clear out now. See you in the gym in less than five."

I started to get undressed. I was thinking this wasn't such a bad deal. Then I looked up, and there was the mirror. You couldn't miss it. You couldn't help but look. At first I sort of had my arms in front of my middle, but then I just dropped my arms and stood there.

Then I got on the scale.

Don't ask me what came over me. But there was nobody there but me. Better to find out in private than at the doctor's. I might as well see how bad it really was.

About 200, I was thinking. If Mr. Bayliss had asked me how bad I thought it had gotten, I'd have said around 200. I tapped the little weights into place: 242. I was officially more than 100 pounds overweight.

I sat down on the scale for a few minutes, and then I got up and put on my sweatpants and T-shirt. And joined the other guys in the gym. They were playing dodgeball. Ah, geez. Anything but dodgeball. There should be a law against that game. It's like legal torture.

Will looked surprised to see me, but I just kept avoiding his eyes.

This guy named Alex and this other guy named Kenny had gym class with us, fifth period. And even though Will and I weren't exactly friends with them, we had a certain amount in common. That is, they weren't exactly jocks, either. Not quite the "it" crowd. So I could sense the four of us trying to look out for each other throughout the regrettably legal viciousness that is dodgeball. Trying to have each other's backs. Kind of a professional courtesy.

All through the game I was thinking I'd have to do something. This had gone far enough. It'd be hard, because I couldn't tell my mother I was going on a diet. She's bigger than me. There's just no way I can say a thing like that without making her feel bad about herself. Without hurting her feelings. Maybe I could say my appetite was off and I didn't even know why.

After dodgeball Will came up to me. "It didn't work?"

"Not exactly. I didn't get a pass. But I do get to shower and change in Mr. Bayliss's office."

"Good deal. Problem solved."

I knew I had a bigger problem than that, though. Thanks to Mr. Bayliss, I was looking it head-on.

When I got home, my mom was standing at the stove. Stirring with a wooden spoon in the big pasta pot.

"Your nose does not deceive you," she said. "I made your favorite dinner."

Fettuccine Alfredo. She makes the noodles from scratch. It's the best, most wicked, most addictive thing anybody has ever eaten. My father used to call it death on a plate. The sauce is made out of half a cup of butter, a whole cup of heavy cream, and a whole cup of Parmesan cheese. I don't even want to think about how many calories it has. Well, you don't. That's the thing. You don't think about it. When you eat fettuccine Alfredo, it means you give up, you don't care about the calories. It's like when you've been flailing around in the water trying to get someone to rescue you, but then you give up and just sink. You stop caring and sink.

I sank hard today. I ate two plates full. Once I got started, I couldn't stop eating. I just stopped caring.

November 6th

Will was standing in front of his locker when I came down the hall this morning. Standing there with his locker door wide open. It's like he was just begging someone to come shove him in and slam the door. I couldn't think what could be so important that he would forget basic safety.

He said, "What's the best news you can possibly think of?"

"Um. Let me see. Amy McPhee wants to go out with me."

"In your dreams, buddy, but this is close. I finally talked my dad into taking us fishing on Saturday."

"Oh. Cool." I was actually a little bit afraid of the ocean. But I was willing to give it a go.

Will and I had a deal, right since we met at the beginning of the school year. He was going to take me out on the
ocean and show me fishing his way, and I was going to take
him up to my uncle Max's cabin and show him fishing
my way.

His way you're out on a twelve-foot metal boat, swaying with the tide, using this tackle where the hooks are like
the size of your hand. Where the line is twenty-five- or
thirty-pound test, and you're wrestling these big sea mon-
sters up out of the deep. Having to use a net or a gaffing
hook just to get them up into the boat without breaking
the line.

My way you're perched at the side of this running
creek, with four-pound test and a pole that swishes back
and forth at the tip when you move it. Waiting for that
special little stutter that says trout. Then reeling in, watching the silver of its belly crisscross through the water before
it breaks the surface in one final jump for freedom. If you
know your stuff you never even need to get your feet wet.

I think I like my kind best, but he swears once I get used
to pulling in the big ones, I'll never go back. I'll get spoiled
and I'll never want to fish for twelve-inch trout again.

That's actually what I'm worried about. I'm worried he
might be right.

He also likes hunting, but I don't think I'm up for that.

About a second later the jocks cruised by, and Will
quick closed the locker before he could get shoved into it.
So he hadn't entirely lost his mind.

Just as they got level with us, all five of them did one of those fish imitations. You know, the kind with your hands up by your face like gills, and your mouth going in a little O. In perfect unison. Almost as though they knew what we'd been talking about. I mean, someone seeing it from the outside might think so. But really, they did this to us almost every day.

Just a run-of-the-mill school of jockfish going by. Taking the opportunity to rag on us as they passed. They thought fishing was hilarious. And that we were total dorks for liking it. Why Will ever talked about fishing out loud in class, I'll never know.

I guess he thinks fishing is cool. Him and just about nobody else.

I heard their laughter echoing back to us all the way down the hall. Even after they turned the corner, I could still hear them laughing.

We sat in the cafeteria, daydreaming. Out loud. To each other.

"My dream," he said, "is to live in a world where Lisa Muller would give me the time of day."

"Dream on," I said. "Besides, she's no Amy McPhee."

"Amy McPhee is beautiful in an obvious sort of way."

I laughed at him, then sucked some milk out of a straw, then laughed at him again. "There is nothing wrong with obvious beauty."

"Maybe not, but still."

Just then somebody passing behind me bonked me on the back of the head with their tray. Hard. I figured it was an accident until I heard somebody laughing. I looked around. It wasn't even the usual suspects. Total strangers, probably seniors. Senseless drive-by cruelty.

The only one who seemed to notice was this girl named Jane, who was sitting with us at the Safety Table. Plain Jane, the cruel ones called her. Sort of in the Kenny and Alex category. She rolled her eyes as a professional courtesy.

"I don't even mean give me the time of day, as in date me," Will said, going on like total strangers hadn't just needlessly assaulted me. I think he was so deep inside his own head that he didn't even see. "I know that's asking too much. I mean literally give me the time of day. Well, no, not literally. I don't mean I'd ask her what time it is. I mean literally just the kind of time you give a stranger. Like I'd say something funny and she'd laugh. She has the greatest laugh. Or even if she just smiled at me. That would be enough. You see, my young Ernie? My goals are realistic. My goals are modest."

I just shook my head at him. I finished my milk, and the straw made a rude sucking sound.

I looked at Lisa. Needless to say, she was not looking at us. She was talking to her friends and to one of the jocks. Either Mike or Dave. Or maybe his name was Rusty. They all kind of mush together in my head. She had long dark hair and dark eyes and a nose that was a little too big. But she was pretty. Will was right about that. Not in the most obvious way. Not like a Hollywood starlet. Not like the curvy blonde you throw at a guy when you want him to say "Oooh" without even thinking. This was something a little more real. She might actually have been real.

"That's it," he said. "I've made up my mind."

"What mind?" I said. But just kidding, not really being mean. You can talk like that when friends know they're friends.

He ignored me. "I've just made a resolution. Someday I will go up to Lisa Muller and say something to make her laugh." He stared off in her direction and sighed. "It's resolved."

Just as he said that, she stood up from her table and picked up her tray.

"Go, tiger," I said.

He just sat. "I have to think of something funny first."

"Right. I get it."

"Besides, I said someday. I definitely did not say today."

A day like yesterday is why Uncle Max gave me this journal. I know it is. I think he figures the little stuff is important, too, but this is the kind of thing you'd put in a journal even if you never had one before. I couldn't even bring myself to write about this yesterday. It was just too long a day and I was too tired and confused. Too upset.

But now it's early Sunday morning and I'm waiting for Uncle Max to drive down from Lemoore to help me with this fish. And I know he's going to ask if I wrote it all out in my journal. I want to be able to say yes. I want to say, I did it just like you told me. Remembering everything everybody said, and putting it down. Also how I felt and what I saw. Like I was writing out a story. So a total stranger could read it and really get what happened.

"But I'll never show it to a total stranger." That's what I said at the time.

He said that's not why. He said it was because later, when I'm a grown-up, I'll look back on it, and I'll be so far removed I'll need all those details to help bring it back. *I'll* be the stranger.

Uncle Max is a writer, and I think he has it in his head that I'll grow up to be one, too. I'm not sure I'm good enough for that. But I'm willing to try what he says.

Anyway, here goes:

We got all the way to the coast, and I found out that Will's father wasn't actually going out on the boat with us. Just me and Will and Sam, Will's little brother. It seemed scarier without a grown-up. I don't know why, really. Grown-ups do stuff wrong all the time. Still. I didn't figure it would just be us.

"I've been out on this boat without my father, like, twenty times."

"Yeah, and he still hasn't caught a legal ling," his father said.

We were standing on the boat ramp, right where it met the sand. This steep concrete ramp with deep ridges, so the trucks can always get traction.

"This'll be the time," Will said. "Besides, I've caught plenty of lings."

"Yeah, plenty of shorts."

"I caught a legal one."

"Hooked a legal one. It's not caught till you get it on the boat."

"Yeah, yeah."

I was too embarrassed to admit I didn't know what a ling is.

All four of us picked up the boat by the stern end. Lifted it off the trailer and set it on the sand. Then Will and his father took the bow end and put that down on the sand, too. Then we all turned it around and pushed it down to the waterline, across this stuff that was more like pebbles than white sand.

"Six hours," his father said. "Keep an eye on your watch. I want this thing landed when I back down the ramp again in six hours."

"Yeah, yeah," Will said.

I got in the front, the seat right behind the bow. Like a metal bench across the narrowest part. Not too comfortable. The waves looked big to me. But I guess I'm not used to judging waves. Sam got in the middle, and Will sat on the stern end, where he could work the outboard motor.

"Ready?" his father asked. He was standing right behind the boat, waiting for a big wave to come along and lift it up a little. He was wearing big rubber boots that came up to his knees. "This one," he said. When it came in, I felt the boat slide sideways. He gave us a big push, and Will grabbed up the oars and rowed like crazy. "Six hours. Don't let me down."

Will's father walked up the pebble-sand to his truck and drove up the ramp and down the road. Meanwhile, Will kept rowing, until we were out beyond the waves. I looked out to the horizon, and a big wave crashed into the bow and caught me in the face. It got my sneakers wet, too. Sam laughed at me. Will told him to shut up.

Will put down the oars and started the motor. Pulling a string, like on a lawn mower engine. He had to do it three or four times. But then it started up, and we went roaring off in the direction of the kelp beds.

"What does he do for six hours while we fish?" I asked Will. I had to yell to be heard over the motor.

"He either goes to the West End bar and plays darts or he goes over to Camozzi's and plays pool."

I could see one other little fishing boat sitting out by the kelp beds, and two or three kayaks. I already felt a little seasick bobbing up over the swells.

After a while Will cut the engine and the boat drifted to a stop in front of the kelp.

Will said, "We'll try here because it's good fishing by the kelp beds. But there might be a drift, so be careful. Really watch your line and the kelp. If you get hung up, half the time you have to cut the line to get it back. Then you lose your leader and your jig. Gets expensive. And look behind you to see if the boat is drifting into the kelp, too."

Sam was tying up his rig. Tying on a swivel and then hooking up a leader that had two big hooks on it, tied up with bright red artificial feathers. I watched him to get the idea of the rig. He looked up and saw me looking. "Thought your dopey friend here already knew how to fish."

Will reached out and knocked Sam in the head. "He's a trout fisherman. Show some respect."

"Ow." Sam went back to tying up, almost like nothing had ever happened. He put a big spoon-shaped jig with a giant treble hook at the end of the leader.

I'd met Will's brother, Sam, once before. I didn't like him. I guess Will didn't, either. He was about twelve. Or maybe eleven, I don't know. And he wasn't an outcast like us. And he wasn't afraid to show off about that.

I tied up the way they did, pulling gear out of Will's tackle box. I could hear the wind whistle, and I watched it flip over bits of kelp sitting on the very top of the water. I looked out to the horizon and saw great blue herons perched on top of the kelp on their long legs, which seemed so weird. Who would've thought it would hold them?

Will handed me a wooden board with frozen squid on it, and a knife. "Put a squid head on your treble hook. Just on one hook. Go in right between the eyes. It stays on better that way. And then cut some small pieces of the tubes to go on your shrimp jig hooks. Higher up."

"But it's frozen solid," I said.

"Doesn't matter. Just break off a head. It'll thaw fast enough in the water. And keep your thumb on the spool when you're unreeling," Will said. "Or the reel will get spinning too fast and you'll have a rat's nest of line to deal with."

I looked down at my pole and at the line. The whole thing looked like something from the land of the giants.

We just sat there for a while, watching our reels as they spooled out. Then I felt my jig hit the bottom.

"Come up three or four cranks off the bottom," Will said, and I did. "Otherwise you'll get snared up."

"Gets expensive," I said.

"Righto," he said. Will actually said things like righto. It's just who he was.

We sat for a while, and I noticed that they popped the tips of their poles up and down now and then, so I did, too.

Will said, "This is my lingcod day. I can feel it."

Sam blew a raspberry. "You'll never get a legal ling. Never. You've got the lingcod curse. He'll either be short, or he'll break the line, or he'll twist off the hook. You've always been cursed for lingcod. What makes you think today will be different?"

"You watch," Will said. "You watch how it'll be different."

We sat without talking awhile longer, and I tried not to think about the motion of the boat on the swells. The swells were so big. We could actually feel the boat roll into the valley after each one. I was scared a big one might break right over the side of the boat. But none did. I was even more afraid to throw up in front of Sam.

Then I saw the tip of Sam's rod stutter, and he yelled out, "First fish!"

"Damn," Will said. "Sam always gets first fish."

He reeled it up and plopped it into the boat at my feet, where it flopped around on my sneakers. It was golden brown, with thick, jagged stripes that were almost flesh-colored, and it had bugged-out eyes.

"It's just a little gopher rockfish," Will said. Like he felt better now.

"It's still first fish."

Not five minutes later Sam reeled in his twin.

"We're moving," Will said.

"But I'm doing good here!" Sam whined back.

"We're moving." And he fired up the engine and veered us over closer to the big rock, sitting out in the middle of nowhere. "This is a better spot," he said when he'd cut the engine and turned the boat to slow it down. "This is where I caught that big ling, right off this rock."

"Hooked it, you mean," Sam said. "If you don't get it up on the boat, you didn't catch it."

"Yeah, yeah."

I've always hated being an only child. I always thought a brother would be the best thing. But, listening to them, I started thinking I might be wrong.

We dropped our jigs in and spooled down. Just sat like that awhile, popping our poles up and down. Then I saw Will pull up on his, but it didn't come up. It just stopped. It just got stuck and wouldn't come up.

"Ha-ha," Sam said. "Will's stuck on the bottom. Great spot to fish all right, Will."

Then the next thing we knew, the tip of Will's rod came down so hard it was curved almost into the water. Like it was trying to get under the boat.

"That ain't the bottom," Will said. His voice was all full of panic, but thrilled, too. "That's a ling."

"How do you know?" I asked.

Sam said, "Loosen the drag, or he'll break the line."

Will said, "I know it! I know how to fish, idiot."

I said, "How do you know it's a ling?"

Sam said, "A ling always feels like you caught the bottom. At first."

Will's face was set hard, and I could tell he was really working to get that fish up. I could see. Now and then the fish would pull back suddenly, and I could hear the zipping sound of four or five feet of line being pulled back off the reel.

Sam said, "You loosened the drag too much."

Will said, "Shut up, idiot. He's coming up."

I looked over the starboard side of the boat, and he was coming up. I saw him. He was huge. Maybe almost as long as the boat was wide, at least my part of the boat. When he got higher up and I really saw what he looked like, I was shocked. No, more than shocked. Scared. "What the hell *is* that?" I yelled.

Will said, "It's a lingcod, what does it look like?"

I didn't say so, but I was thinking it looked like the devil. It was dark, dark green, with mottled sides and a fin all down its long back that made it look like a dragon. And eyes that slanted in toward each other and looked so fierce it was more like a monster than a fish. And it came up with its mouth open, and it had teeth. Actual sharp, pointy teeth. It was like pure evil, only with fins.

"Sam!" Will yelled. "The net. Get the net."

Sam jumped for the net, but the long handle was caught under the big loops of the boat's towrope. He dove down to the boat's floor and tried to get it untangled.

Will yelled, "If you make me lose this fish, Sam—"

"Swim it back and forth! Don't let the line slack!"

"I know how to fish, idiot!"

I heard that sound again, of line being pulled out from the spool. "Damn," Will said. "He's pulling the boat closer to the kelp. Damn. Damn! Get that damn net, Sam. He's going to get tied up in the kelp. Oh, damn! Damn it. He's in the kelp. He's all wrapped up in the kelp." I saw Will adjust the drag again. Tighten it this time. He reeled in slowly, and the boat moved over a little closer to the fish.

Sam said, "You'll break the line!"

Will said, "Shut up, idiot!" He reached into his tackle

box and pulled out a yellow nylon stringer. Then he reeled in a little more and got even closer to the fish. He leaned over the starboard side of the boat, reaching for it. The boat tilted dangerously close to the water. But he couldn't reach. He reeled in a little bit more.

The fish was holding still, the line wrapped around the kelp just barely under the surface of the water. Only his tail swished back and forth. His mouth still gaped wide open, showing those horrifying teeth.

Will reached over, and he was close enough this time. He reached down and stuck the metal-covered end of the stringer through the fish's open gills. But it didn't come out his mouth the way I know Will meant it to. And he damn sure wasn't going to stick his fingers in with those teeth. So he yelled to Sam to get him the pliers. Meanwhile, I watched the starboard edge of the boat and the surface of the water. They were even more dangerously close together.

"He's got to be thirty inches, easy," Will said. Sam said nothing. Which I took to mean he was probably thirty inches, easy.

Sam handed over the pliers, and Will reached them into the ling's mouth and caught the end of the stringer. Caught it on the second try. He pulled it out with a bragging yell: "Ha-ha!" Threaded it through the ring on the other end. Then he sat back and pulled hard, and it slipped into place. Just like a stringer is supposed to do. Tightened down like a leash, wrapped through the gill and out the mouth. But this leash would be pretty hard to break. Will sat back and sneered at Sam. Meanwhile, he wrapped the end of the stringer three or four times around his hand.

"Told you this was my lingcod day. Told you my luck was about to change."

He pulled hard on the stringer, but he still couldn't pull the fish out of the kelp. He pulled a second time, and the starboard side of the boat rocked disastrously close to the water. He even tried cutting his line, but it was really wrapped around the kelp. It didn't come free on the fish's end. Will pulled even harder.

"Hey, watch out, idiot," Sam yelled. "You'll sink us."

"I am *not* losing this fish. Ernie, hand me that knife."

I grabbed the bait board and handed Will the knife. He used it to point in the direction of his brother's face. "This never would've happened if you'd gotten me the net when I asked for it."

"It was tangled up."

"You didn't try hard enough. Because you don't *want* my luck to change." Will pulled as hard as he could on the stringer, then leaned over the starboard side of the boat with the knife, grabbing strands of kelp, pulling them close to the boat, and cutting them. The harder he pulled, the closer the side of the boat got to the water.

Sam started reeling in so his line wouldn't get snared up in the kelp. I was about to do the same, but I never got that far.

I looked up and saw a really scary swell coming our way. The boat had turned around now, so the starboard side was facing the swells. And the next swell was a really big one. And the side of the boat and the water were only about an inch apart.

"Will, sit up," I said. "Sit up a minute. There's a big swell coming."

"I've almost got it."

Sam looked up and saw what I saw. But he didn't say anything to Will. He took it out on me instead. "Fat Boy, sit on the port side!"

I did, and it helped a little. But maybe not enough.

Will sat up and hit Sam in the head. "Leave him alone," he said. Then he leaned over to cut the last piece of kelp.

"Will, sit up! Now!"

"I've got it," he said. "I've got it." He started to sit up. But as he did, he lifted the fish into the boat, and that brought the starboard side down even farther. Right to the waterline.

That's when the swell hit.

It washed so much water into the boat that it slid me down to the low side, and I just kept going. Right off the boat and into the water. I closed my eyes and held my breath. The water was shockingly cold. I don't even know how to describe how cold it was. Like being dipped in a glass of ice water. It hurt. It felt almost like being burned. Not exactly, but a little. Really hot and really cold feel a little bit the same. They both sting almost the same way.

At first I just kept going down, but then I slowed and headed for the surface. There is one thing to be said for fat. It floats. My head bobbed up into air. I still had the rod in my hands. I couldn't lose Will's rod.

I looked around. The boat was gone. Nowhere. Worse yet, nobody. No Will, no Sam. Just me and a great blue heron standing on one leg on the kelp bed. Then I saw one of the wooden oars floating near my head, and the blue-and-white bait cooler bobbing on the water. I saw all three bright orange life jackets. I tried to dog-paddle over to one.

Just then Will's head came up, and he raised his right hand to show me the end of the stringer, still wrapped around it. "It's okay," he said. "I still got him."

My mouth fell open, and a little salt water lapped in, and I had to spit it out again. "*Okay? It's okay?* Dude, we sank your father's boat!"

We just looked at each other for a minute. Treaded water. The cold was going from painful to numb. Something banged into the back of my head. When I turned around, I saw it was the other oar.

"Oh, this is bad," Will said. Then his big fish pulled so hard that Will's head disappeared.

When he bobbed up again, I said, "Yeah. No shit this is bad. Where's Sam?"

I know it's weird. But I really hadn't thought of it until right when I said it.

"I don't know," Will said. But he didn't sound too concerned. "When did you last see him?"

"Before that swell hit. Can he swim?"

"Oh, hell yeah. He can swim circles around both of us. He's a competition swimmer." Will turned all around, looking. "Sam!" We just waited. "Messing with us, that's where he is. Behind that rock, I bet. He's fine."

I thought I saw a dark look pass over his face, but I might've been wrong. Everything was dark just then. Who could tell one dark thing from another?

I paddled over to one of the life jackets. Slipped it on. Threw another one to Will. It was hard to buckle it, though. I had to hold the pole between my knees and adjust the straps way out, and my fingers didn't work right. But I got it buckled. Finally. When I looked up, Will had his on, too. He had a look of true panic on his face.

"What am I gonna tell my dad? We lost everything. Not even just the boat. The outboard motor. All the rods, all the tackle."

"Well, you've got both oars," I said. "And the cooler, and the life vests. And this rod." I held up my right hand. I couldn't even feel I had anything in my right hand, but I held it up, and the rod was still there.

Then something weird happened. If there really is a God, I think he's a funny guy. I think he has a sense of humor. Maybe at my expense. The tip of the rod jerked three or four times.

"You got something," Will said.

I tried to reel up. But my hands didn't work very well. They were really numb and frozen by then. But eventually I got it up where I could see it.

"Hey," Will said. "You caught a nice red."

"Yeah, that's a great consolation. Lost the boat, caught a nice red."

"Well, at least you didn't get skunked."

It was red all right. Bright orangey red. I didn't even know colors like that existed in the fish world. By my standards as a trout fisherman, it was a big fish. Compared to Will's ling, it was tiny. It hardly mattered at all.

"Give it to me," he said. "I'll put it on the stringer."

I went through the motions with him. But some part of me felt like I was watching this whole thing from above. Standing outside myself. Thinking how weird it was to even still be caring about the fish. Treading water, probably eighty feet above the boat, putting the last fish on the stringer. Like nothing had happened.

I reeled the line the rest of the way in and hooked one of the treble hooks on one of the pole's guides, then reeled up tight so the hook would stay. I didn't want to catch myself on it. And I was determined to get to shore with that rod. It was the only piece of equipment I was responsible for. No way was I letting it go.

I shoved the handle of it into the waistband of my jeans.

I looked up and saw people standing on the beach watching us. "I hope they call somebody," I said. "I hope they call it in. Call 911. Maybe they'll call the Coast Guard or Search and Rescue or whatever."

Will just swam away. I could tell he was going to look on the other side of the rock. I got scared, thinking what if he was wrong and nobody was there. But he said the kid could swim.

Will's head came out from behind the rock again. "He probably swam to shore just to show us he can get there before we even start."

"We'd have seen him."

"I saw him," he said. "Right there."

"Where?" I looked, but all I saw was ocean.

"I just saw his head pop up, just there. I know I did." He sounded like it was really important that I believe him. Or maybe even that he believe himself.

"Hoo-boy, I hope you're right. Will, I can't swim all the way to shore."

"You don't have much choice," he said.

I think we were about a fifth of the way back to shore when we got rescued. Maybe we weren't even that far.

It was Fish and Game who came and got us. I think somebody put a call over the radio, and Fish and Game was close by. Two guys on a sort of pontoon boat. But it had a motor and it was fast.

They pulled us up and on board, but they both had to grab hold of me and pull, which was just so humiliating.

One of the guys had really short hair, like his head had been shaved but now he had five o'clock shadow. The other guy was wearing this bandanna on his head like a do-rag. Bandanna Man said, "I know you kids can't have been out here on your own."

"No, sir," Will said. "My brother was out here, too. We think he swam ashore." Then he pulled the stringer up.

The shaved guy whistled. "Nice ling. Must be over thirty inches. Man, that's a beauty. You catch that, son?"

"No, sir," Will said. "My friend Ernie did. I caught this red snapper."

I looked at Will but he wouldn't catch my eye.

Bandanna Man said, "Who's the grown-up in charge here?"

Will said, "Well, my dad. He was gonna pick us up in six hours."

The two men looked at each other. Then they started up the motor and we raced at the shore. Got there like ten times faster than it took us to get out. They ran the motor until the boat slid right up on the sand.

There was a crowd of people waiting for us. Well, a small crowd. Maybe a dozen. And an ambulance parked on the road, but we didn't need that. We were fine. And a sheriff's car with the red lights spinning.

Bandanna Guy yelled out to the crowd. He said, "Anybody see another boy come ashore?"

Everybody shook their heads.

I sat on the end of that boat ramp with this stiff gray blanket wrapped around me, but I was still freezing. I could feel my teeth knocking together when they chattered. I tried so hard to stop shaking, but I just couldn't stop.

I could still feel the motion of the swells when I closed my eyes.

The Fish and Game guys were back out on the water, looking for Sam, and there was another boat out there now, too. Some kind of Search and Rescue boat, with a diver on board. And a helicopter kept buzzing back and forth over the water.

I was thinking, I must be in hell. This must be hell. I'm cold and miserable, I'm starving hungry, Will and I are in deep trouble, we still haven't found Sam, and I have no way to get home. And it just kept going on, for what felt like hours. I was thinking, If I ever go to hell for real, which I hope I don't, it couldn't be any worse than this.

A minute later the sheriff's deputy came walking down the boat ramp. "I found your father," he said. "But he's in no condition to drive you boys home. You got any other options on a ride?"

"We could call my mother," I said. I gave him the number. I wanted to call her myself, but he had to do it from his car, through dispatch. "Tell her I'm okay," I said as he walked up the ramp. "Don't forget. She worries."

"All mothers worry," he said.

I looked over at Will. "I'm staying," he said. "Here. Don't forget your fish."

He took the red off the stringer and handed me the stringer, lingcod and all.

"I don't get it."

"You think I want my father to know I was thinking about not losing a big fish while his boat was sinking? That I made sure I kept hold of the ling but I'm not sure what happened to Sam?"

I took the ling. Held it out at arm's length. It was still marginally alive. It still had teeth. It still looked like the devil. And, sure enough, the minute it came up from the deep, everything had gone straight to hell.

When she was finally ready to take a breath from bawling me out, my mother left me home and went to get takeout. It was such a relief. I was trying to shut up and just let her get it out of her system. But I felt like it was never going to end.

"Get sushi," I said, because I like California rolls, and they're not too fattening.

"Honey, we can't afford sushi every time. I'll get McDonald's."

I sighed and drew myself a hot bath. I figured it was the only way I would ever get warm again. I'm not weird. This'll sound weird, but I'm not. I drew a bubble bath. There's a method to my madness. It's impossible to see your body through all those bubbles. All through this, something in the back of my head kept saying, Sam.

I took the phone into the bathroom with me and set it on the bath mat. I just stared at it the whole time I soaked. But it never made a sound.

After I finally felt warm again, I went into the kitchen and stared at that enormous dead devil-fish sitting on some old newspaper on the counter. That sea monster. It looked like it was staring back at me. Creepy. I had no idea what to do with it.

Peaches was walking back and forth under the counter, sniffing. Good thing she has really short legs. She could never get up on that counter.

I know how to fillet a fish. If a trout is twelve inches or under, I usually cook it whole. But if it's a big one, fourteen inches or more, I fillet it. But this guy . . . I took my fillet knife out of the drawer and held it up to the fish. It wouldn't even reach all the way through to the spine. I couldn't figure out where to start. I was tempted to throw it in the outside trash. But it's a crime to waste a big fish like that. Any fish. I'm not big on the idea of sin, but if there was ever a sin, it's to kill an animal and then not even eat it.

I called Uncle Max. Thinking, Sam.

I said, "Uncle Max, I caught this big, giant lingcod, like over thirty inches, and I don't even know how to fillet it, and I was wondering if you could drive down tomorrow and help me."

He said, "Oh, had a good day, huh?"

I said, "No. It was horrible. It was the worst day ever. This big swell sank the boat, and we had to be rescued, and Mom is royally pissed that we went out on a boat without a grown-up, and we still don't know where Will's little brother is." Halfway through saying it, I started to cry. I hate to cry. Hate it. Even when I'm all alone. In front of somebody, it's the worst. But if I was going to cry in front of anybody, at least it was Uncle Max.

"Oh," he said. "I guess that explains why you want me to drive down. Instead of just telling you how to fillet it over the phone."

"I guess," I said. It was almost like he was trying to get me to say I needed help. Which is a really hard thing for me. But he was right, of course. I was really asking him to drive down because he was my uncle Max. Sometimes you just need your uncle Max.

"Okay. Will do. Just gut it and put it in the fridge, and I'll leave as soon as I wake up in the morning."

My mother came back in with three bags from the fast-food place. Scary to think what she ordered wouldn't even fit into two bags.

I said, "Thanks, Uncle Max." And got off the phone.

While she laid it all out on the table, I slit the belly of the fish and pulled the guts out onto the newspaper. Considering the size of the fish, there weren't a lot of guts. More like just what a trout would have. Or, in this case, a dozen trout. I used my knife to cut them away at the ends and right behind the head, and then I stuck the front end of the fish in the kitchen sink and scraped out the blood vein as best I could. Rinsed it inside and cleaned it out with four or five paper towels. Wrapped the fish in plastic wrap, round and round until it was all covered.

"Come on, Ernie," my mother said. "It's going to get cold."

"I'll be right there."

But I wasn't right there. I had to find space for that monster in the fridge. This was no small task, believe me. We have lots of food in our fridge. I had to move things around. Stack things on top of other things. Take out a bunch of stuff like ketchup and mustard and salad dressing and jam and jelly, stuff that would survive on the counter until morning. Then I managed to wedge the fish in on a lower shelf, but I had to stack some stuff on top of it.

I balled up the guts in the paper and ran it out real quick to the outside trash. I knew it would stink by morning. I also knew Peaches might knock over the inside trash in the night.

When I got back, my mom was sitting at the table, not eating. Just letting her food get cold. I sat down. She'd gotten me two Big Macs, a giant fries, a supersize soda, and one of those deep-fried apple pies. I was so hungry from not having eaten since breakfast. I never even got to eat my lunch. It ended up at the bottom of the ocean.

"Why didn't you start?" I said, picking up a Big Mac.

"Put it down," she said. I did. I didn't know why. I just knew it was no day to go pushing my luck. "Before we eat, we're going to say a prayer for that little boy. What's his name?"

"Sam." It was the first time I'd said it out loud for so long. Sam.

"Right. We're going to say a prayer that Sam Manson is okay. And that they find him before it gets dark."

We sat there in silence for a minute. Our heads bowed. I don't know if I should call what I was doing praying. I'm not so sure about the whole God thing. I'm not saying there isn't one, but I don't know. And if there is, I'm not sure I like him. I guess I shouldn't think that, but it's true. But I wanted Sam to get found real bad. So I hoped real hard. Maybe that's all a prayer is. Just hoping real hard that things turn out okay.

I cheated once and looked up at my mom. She just got her hair cut short. I don't like it. But I keep saying I do. I want to be supportive. A lot of her weight is in her face. She has very big cheeks. Usually they're pretty red. Yesterday even more so. I worry about her. I think it's a blood pressure thing. I quick looked away again.

Then we picked up our food, and I took a big bite of burger and ate four fries all at once. They were really cold, but I didn't care. I wanted to get numb. I wanted to eat so much that I couldn't feel. I didn't want to feel anything at all. There was nothing good to be felt. Any feelings I had were going to be bad ones.

Now and then I glanced at the kitchen phone, sitting on the wall. But it never made a sound. It never told me anything about Sam.

By about nine o'clock at night, I just couldn't stand it anymore. I had to know. But I was afraid to call Will's house. What if his father answered? What if Will was being punished in some horrible way and couldn't come to the phone?

I'm not big at talking these things out, but I got so twisted up and confused that I actually asked my mom what to do. I could tell by the look on her face that she couldn't stand not knowing, either.

"I will call Will's father. That's more appropriate. Besides, I want to give him a piece of my mind."

I just died inside. So much for the idea that this day couldn't get any worse. This is why I never ask advice from a grown-up. In case that doesn't go without saying.

I sat at the kitchen table, frozen in my misery, while she made the call. Then, worse yet, somebody answered.

I heard her say, "Mr. Manson?"

Then, "Yes, this is Lila Boyd. Ernie's mother? I just wanted to know if they ever found your son Sam."

Then, "Oh, they did? That's just wonderful!"

But the wonderful didn't last for long.

For the next five minutes or so—which felt like an hour, by the way—a string of little comments from my mom. With long, long silences in between. *Long* silences. Ugly silences. Horrible silences.

"Oh. Oh, no. . . . Oh, that's just terrible. . . . Oh, I'm so sorry. . . . You must feel just terrible. . . . Why didn't he . . . ? Oh, he did. . . . Oh my. . . . That does give you an awful lot on your mind, yes. . . . Well, I don't know, Mr. Manson. That's really not for me to say. . . . Well, I guess that's up to a judge to decide. . . . Of course. . . . I'm so sorry for your loss. . . . How is Will holding up? . . . I see. . . . Well, I'm so sorry, Mr. Manson. We'll keep your family in our prayers."

Believe it or not, all through this, I still held out hope. Or denial. Whatever you want to call it. Will said the kid could swim. I kept thinking she'd hang up and say he was in the hospital or something. Something not really so bad as all that.

She hung up the phone and started to cry. The denial broke up like a thin crust of ice when you step on it.

Worse yet, when *I* step on it. My stomach just got heavier and heavier. And it felt like everything was being sucked out of my world. Whatever I used to half-ass survive on. Gone. And the inside of my brain got more and more tingly, like the world was getting farther and farther away.

"I don't get it," I said. "Why didn't he just swim?"

"He got caught on his own hook. Two of the hooks on his . . . what do you call it?"

"Treble?"

"Yes. Treble. Two of the hooks went through his jeans. And the line was tangled on some part of the boat. Or pinned under it or something. I guess he wasn't strong enough to break the line."

"Why didn't he just take off his jeans? Come up without them?"

"They think he tried. His jeans were down around his knees when they found him. And he had one boot off. I guess he couldn't get his jeans off over those big boots. And then I guess he just . . . ran out of time."

We both just sat there, for a long time, not saying anything. I had this image in my head of Sam floating in the water, at the end of his own rig. Tethered down to the boat. Right underneath us. The whole time we were putting on our life vests. Putting that red on the stringer. That whole time, the kid was down there. Right underneath us. Running out of time.

"You didn't exactly give him a piece of your mind," I

said. I was surprised I said it. Surprised I said anything. It wasn't a complaint. I totally didn't want her to.

"Well, that's hardly the time. When he's just lost his younger boy. Besides, he has much bigger problems than me. He just got out on bail. They arrested him for child endangerment. He might have to go to jail."

I got busy wondering what Will would do if his only parent went to jail. Where he would live. If he'd have to go back to L.A. If I was about to lose my best friend. While I was doing that, my mom started to cry again.

She didn't even know Sam. I knew him. Why wasn't I crying? Even though I hated to cry. Still, maybe I should. Maybe I was being totally the wrong kind of person. Maybe it was really bad not to cry.

"When I think how that could have been you," she said. Then she hurried over and smothered me in a hug. Crushed me. "You're all I've got, Ernie. I just don't know what I'd do." She didn't let go, either. She just kept me there. Smothered. Crushed. Suffering. I guess hell lasts a long time. An eternity, they say.

I felt almost like my two Big Macs and my mountain of fries were about to make a return appearance. But it was like that day in Mr. Bayliss's office. It didn't get bad enough to throw up. But it never really went away, either.

Later that night I went online to check my e-mail. Hoping I had something from Will. I didn't, though. I really, really wanted to know if he was okay. Well, that's stupid. Of course he wasn't okay. I knew that. I guess I mean I needed to know *how* okay he wasn't.

I just kept sitting there, staring at the screen, running send-and-receive cycles. Hoping this would be the time. It was almost one in the morning. But I knew I'd never sleep if I went to bed.

All of a sudden I got that jingle that means someone is trying to instant-message me. It made me jump. It was Will.

The message said: welcome to life in the manson family

That's how Will writes on the Internet. No caps, no punctuation. All lowercase. About a month ago I started doing mine in all uppercase, sort of to make fun of him. I don't think he caught on to why. It just sort of stuck.

I wrote, OH MY GOD ARE YOU OKAY WHAT DID HE SAY TO YOU

Then I waited. Too long, I thought.

you wont believe it

TRY ME

he said sam was all i had
he said sam was all i had
since your mother left us
i just gave him this look

like dad like think what
youre saying finally i
said what the hell am i

WHAT DID HE SAY

nothing just looked at his
shoes

THATS HORRIBLE WILL

thats life in the manson
family

I didn't think he should make a joke about a thing like
this. But I didn't know how to say so.

ARE YOU GONNA BE OKAY

the last thing i said to
him was he was an idiot
i hit him and called him
an idiot last words nice
huh

HE KNOWS YOU LOVED HIM

how could he know that i
didnt even know i loved
him i thought i hated him
i did hate him right up
until that swell hit

While I was sitting there trying to think of what to say at a moment like that, he typed: promise me you wont tell anyone

WHAT

i said promise you wont
tell

NO I MEAN TELL WHAT

that it was my fault

IT WASNT YOUR FAULT WILL

promise you wont tell
that i was the one who
capsized the boat and we
didnt even wonder where
he was until longer than

it takes for a person to
drown

IT WASNT YOUR FAULT IT WAS
A FREAK ACCIDENT

promise

YEAH, I typed. I PROMISE

I still couldn't get to sleep. I kept thinking how horrible that would feel. To be holding your breath, trying to get the hooks out of your jeans. Trying to break the line. All the time knowing you're running out of time. And then, when you finally do, what then? You have to breathe. You can't not breathe any longer. So I guess you give up and breathe water? It just seems like the most awful, horrible way to go.

Sometimes I would almost get to sleep, but I'd have these dreams like the kind you have when you're half awake. Really vivid stuff. In one I saw Sam's body floating over the boat, his eyes open. A few last bubbles coming up out of his mouth. And then all of a sudden it was me. I sat up really fast, and Peaches was up on the bed with me, and she jumped. I didn't want to go back to sleep, but after a while I did. I dreamed I saw the lingcod sneaking up on me from around my bedroom chair. Swimming in the air, coming after me.

After that I sat up and wrote all this down in my journal. It wasn't even quite three o'clock in the morning when I started. Usually I write in my journal for about a half hour. But now it's after five-thirty.

I'm not even going to try to get back to sleep.

Uncle Max came at ten o'clock this morning. Woke me up. So much for never getting back to sleep. But still, I'd only had two or three hours, and my eyes felt like they had sand in them, and my stomach was a little upset. It has been since yesterday. It still is. I'm beginning to think it always will be.

Peaches woke me, actually. When she heard the sound of his truck. I opened my eyes and she was up on the bed, trying to get a look out the window. Making little noises in her throat—*grrrffff*—with her tail going like mad. Peaches loves Uncle Max.

I sat up and tried to get my brain working. Then I went downstairs and let him in.

He looked me up and down. "Am I disturbing your beauty sleep?"

"I had a little trouble sleeping last night."

"Understandable."

Uncle Max is around sixty-five years old. Twenty years older than my mom. He's really her half brother, from when their father—my grandfather—was married before. So he's sort of like a grandfather to me. I call him my uncle, and he is, but he fits in that grandfather space. I got rooked on real grandparents. All four died before I was born.

He still has all his hair, but it's snow-white, and his beard is white and bristly. He reminds me of the pictures I've seen of Ernest Hemingway. He has this special way of talking, like an actor. Very dramatic. I always picture him holding a human skull and talking right to it, like in a Shakespeare play.

Peaches was wiggling all around his feet.

"I heard about what happened with the other boy."

"Oh. How?"

"Lila called me. So do I need to properly ream you out for going out on a tiny boat in big swells with just another couple of kids? It *was* pretty damn stupid. Or did Lila cover that sufficiently already?"

"Oh, she gave it to me good, all right."

"Figures. Lila does like to beat a subject to death."

"Hey. That's my mother you're talking about."

"Yeah, and she's my baby sister, too, and I love her to pieces, but does she beat a subject to death or doesn't she? I ask you."

I felt a little smile at the corner of my mouth. What a weird feeling. I thought I might never smile again.

"Introduce me to your new friend," Uncle Max said.

At first I thought he meant Will. But he already met Will. "Huh?"

"The fish, dense boy. The fish."

"Oh. Right." Some friend.

We worked together to pull it out of the fridge and take off the plastic wrap.

"Now, that," Uncle Max said, "is one truly beautiful beast."

"You're kidding."

"No, I am not kidding. It's magnificent. You don't think so?"

"I think it looks like a monster."

"Well, it's fierce. It's a big, ferocious predator. But ferocity can be beautiful."

"Hum. Wow. I don't know." But I was really trying to look at it his way. I was really trying to see beauty in that fish. But the ugliness of yesterday got in the way. They just stayed all tangled up together in my head.

"Well, *I* think so, anyway. Get me your fillet knife. I'll show you how this is done. We may have to put it on newspapers on the floor. I don't think the counter will be big enough. So hold tight to that dog." He looked down at Peaches, and so did I. Those little white curls, and those stubby legs. Like a poodle with some dachshund or basset or both. Silly but cute. "Oh, all right, *hello*, Peaches." He always says it the same way, kind of grudgingly. And Peaches always falls all over herself with joy. "Why does that dog like me? I never give her the time of day."

But Uncle Max likes Peaches right back. He just doesn't like to admit it.

While he was filleting the fish, while I was holding tight to the wiggling dog, he said, "Tell me all about how it felt to catch this beauty."

All of a sudden it got hard to swallow. And my gut tingled the way it did when I was in trouble. "Well, at first it just felt like I was snared up on the bottom."

"Uh-huh. I see, I see. Then what?"

"Um, I don't know. Then I reeled it in."

"How did you get it into the boat without breaking the line?"

"Oh. Sam had a net."

"Sam—that's the boy who died?"

He looked up at me. I never answered. I just looked right into his eyes and thought maybe he knew. Maybe he saw right through me. I didn't know what else to say about how it felt to catch this fish. How would I know? So I said nothing at all.

"Well, I was hoping for a romping good fish story, and that one sucked, but I understand. It was a rough day and you don't care to talk about it. Fair enough. Make yourself useful, then. Fire up that deep fryer and cut up some French fries. I'll make my famous beer batter. Now don't give me that look. I'm not corrupting you. It's only a little beer, and the alcohol cooks away anyway. I'm going to make us the biggest, most golden brown mountain of fish-and-chips you ever saw. And I'll lay you odds we still won't have polished off half of this beauty."

While he talked, I was busy looking at the half-filleted fish. Trying to see beauty.

We sat down to lunch, and I took a bite of the fish. Carefully. Like I half expected it to bite me back or something. It was terrific. Hot and crispy outside and really fluffy and moist and fresh inside. Just fell apart in my mouth. I wolfed down two pieces before my mom broke the silence.

"So, Max," she said, and I could already smell trouble. "Did you have a talk with Ernie about things?"

"Yes. I did. And we're done with such things. He's heard enough now."

"I hope you're right. After all, he could have been killed. Going out all alone—"

He cut her off in mid-sentence. "He was there, Lila. He knows how dangerous it was. It scared him more than it could ever scare you. You want to keep reaming him out for it so he'll think twice before doing something like that again. But he'll never in his life face a dangerous situation without feeling the fear of that day. You don't have to put the fear of God in him, Lila. God installed it directly. Yesterday. Now it's time to show him some support. He's had a trauma. He needs comforting."

At first she said nothing at all. Just shoveled in a few French fries. Then she said, "I suppose you're right, Max. As usual." She sounded hurt.

He reached over and put his hand on top of hers on the table. "I know you're just trying to protect the boy and take care of him. But take care of his insides, too. Just because he survived doesn't mean he's okay."

She nodded.

"Speaking of which," he said, turning his attention back to me, "how's your friend Will doing with his insides?"

"Not good," I said.

My mother looked up suddenly. "You talked to him? When did you talk to him?"

"Just a little bit on the Internet last night. I think we both had trouble sleeping."

Then the table went quiet again. Just when I wanted it not to. I wanted to talk some more about Will, and how he wasn't okay. But I couldn't. Because I couldn't tell anybody what he'd said to let me know he wasn't okay. I was sworn to secrecy. So I just sat there and said nothing.

I looked at that big platter of fish in the middle of the

table. All golden brown and steamy. And I thought, Uncle Max did it again. He taught me to see beauty in that fish. It didn't look like the devil at all to me now. Now that it was beer-battered and fried to perfection, it looked really magnificent.

I took two more pieces.

Uncle Max helped me get the other half of the fish into the freezer. He cut it into serving-size pieces—big servings, our house servings—and handed each one to me, and I wrapped them in plastic wrap and put them all in a giant ziplock freezer bag.

"Should I leave you with my recipe for beer batter?"

"Uh, no. No thanks, Uncle Max. It was delicious. But I think with the other half I should . . . you know . . . bake it or something." He didn't say anything, so I felt like I had to. I just had to spit it out. "I'm trying to lose weight."

When I looked up, he was looking right into my face. He'll do that sometimes, just look at you for a long time before he says anything. Like he's trying to work something out. "Good for you, Ernie. My apologies. If I'd known, I'd have fixed lunch some other way."

"Oh, no, it's okay. It was delicious. Besides, you didn't know."

"I'm surprised Lila didn't tell me."

"Well. That's because she . . ." I just kind of ran out of steam and never finished.

"Because she . . . ," he said, trying to lead me to it.

"Doesn't know."

He put down the fish fillet and the knife and turned and looked at me full on. I wanted to sink right through the floor. "Why have you not told your mother? Isn't that pretty key? She can't support you if she doesn't know you need support."

"I know."

"Why, then?"

I really, really wanted to be somewhere else entirely. I looked down at my shoes. Peaches was down there, staring up at the fish fillets. Licking her lips, like she could eat the good smells. "You remember how my dad was. Always criticizing her."

"Yeah. So?"

"This would be like criticizing. Like telling her she should do something, too."

"Nonsense. If you don't want to be like your dad, don't criticize her. But tell her what you've decided for yourself."

"I don't want to make her feel bad about herself."

"Stop trying to fix the world, Ernie. She makes her decisions, you make yours. She's a big girl. Let her feelings be her business. *Tell* her."

He handed me the last two pieces of fish and washed his hands in the sink, and I knew he was going to go. I wished he wouldn't. But it was a long drive, and he probably had things to do.

I walked him to the door.

"Thanks for driving all this way, Uncle Max."

"Yeah. Well. You know you're my favorite nephew." This is a little running joke we have. I'm an only child, and Uncle Max and my mom don't have any other brothers or sisters. In other words, I'm his *only* nephew.

A couple of steps out the door he stopped and turned around. "Oh. I know what I forgot to say. Take good care of your friend Will for a while. He needs a lot of attention right now, and he's probably not getting it at home. Hey. Want to go up to the cabin for Christmas vacation? Just the two of us?"

"I'd love to. But I bet Mom wouldn't like it. She'll want me to be home with her on Christmas."

"I'll talk to her." He turned and walked toward his truck again. Then he stopped, snapped his fingers. Turned around. "I almost forgot the most important question."

"Yes. I wrote it all down in my journal. Almost three hours' worth."

He pointed in the general direction of my nose. "Good boy."

Then he jumped into the truck, and he was gone.

I've been bad about writing in my journal. Really bad. It's been ages. After that big marathon writing thing, where I practically got a hand cramp putting down all the details of the worst twenty-four hours of my life, well . . . After that I'd look at the thing and really not want to touch it. Kind of like I feel about the leftover lingcod in our freezer. Just doesn't look all that appetizing.

But stuff has been happening. It's just sort of quiet stuff. Literally. At first I had no idea what to say about it. But Will kind of cleared it up today. Kind of put words to it and made it real.

He's been back at school for around six days.

I was really braced, waiting for someone to beat him over the head with it. But instead everybody just got sort of . . . quiet. I'd walk into a class with him, and whoever was in the room before us would just clam up. The silence got pretty heavy. It was like some kind of radio waves, following us everywhere we went.

The first one of each class was hard, because the teacher always asked him to stay a minute after class. Then he'd stand by their desks looking helpless, and they'd say something meant to be supportive. "I am so, so sorry about what happened to your brother, Will. We're all holding a good thought for your family." Some crap like that. Meanwhile, I could feel the waves of misery pouring off him. But there wasn't much I could do to help. You can put yourself in front of a knife or a gun. For a buddy you just might. But how do you put yourself in front of somebody who thinks they're being nice?

Why is it so much harder when it's him getting hurt? That's harder for me than when they hurt me. Me, I just figure, Hell, I'm tough. I can take it. But having to hurt on his behalf. Man. That's a tough one.

So I'd just stand there like a dork, ten steps back, like I could dive in and stop the bleeding when it was over. But I couldn't. That's the problem. I couldn't.

We'd just move on to the next class. And the minute we did, more silence. It even happened in the halls. This floating bubble of silence that walked with us. If we slowed down, so did the silence. It was like something out of science fiction. It's almost hard to explain.

I do have to say, though, there was one girl who was actually nice. Her name is Kara, and she's popular. And in spite of that popularity, she actually took the time to treat Will like a human being. To look him right in the eye and say, "It's terrible what happened, and I'm really sorry."

But by that time Will was just so numb. I don't think he realized what a huge thing had just happened.

Neither one of us talked about it. None of it. Not about what happened, and not about what's been happening since. Not even with each other.

Then, today, we were walking home from school, because the bus is pretty brutal. Will looked over at me, and I knew in my gut he was going to talk about it. I don't even know how I knew. I just did. I guess I'm getting pretty good at reading silences.

He said, "Remember when people used to talk?"

"Yeah. I guess so."

"Sometimes not exactly *to* me. But at least they talked *about* me. At least they talked in my presence. It's like the aliens came and stole all our sound."

"It's been weird."

"I don't just mean at school. You should try it at my house. My father not only won't talk to me, he won't look at me. It's like I'm not even there. I start to feel like I'm not even there. Hey."

He stopped walking. It took me a couple of steps to

notice. I turned around, expecting him to catch up with me. But he didn't. So I walked back to where he was standing.

"Hey what?"

"Maybe I'm not."

"Not what?"

"There."

I figured he was kidding. I hoped he was kidding. Hell, I prayed he was kidding. I had to act like I was sure he was. Anything else would be too weird. I reached out and pinched him on the arm. Pretty hard.

"Ow," he said, rubbing his arm.

"Congratulations. You're there."

He just kept standing there with that confused look on his face. "Maybe you're the only one who sees me."

"Okay. Okay. You're seriously freaking me out. You have officially begun to freak me out."

"You're the only one who even looks at me."

"Dude," I said. "Think what you're saying. If they didn't see you come into a room, how would they know to suddenly go all quiet?"

"Maybe they just feel . . . like . . . this big, spooky wind blow through."

"Okay. Freaking out. Please don't get weird on me. You're kidding. Right? Please say you're kidding."

He looked up at me, and it seemed like the evil curse was suddenly lifted. "Yeah. Yeah, I'm kidding. Of course I am."

We started to walk again. But I didn't feel all better. I still felt a little shaken up. Especially when he added one final word. Real quiet. But there it was.

"Mostly."

I'm really starting to worry about Will.

November 28th

This morning when I got to the kitchen table my mom wasn't around. She must've been getting ready for work.

I poured myself a bowl of cereal. Put the milk carton out on the table. Then I saw I'd set the carton right on top of something. So I picked it up again. There was a little clipping from the newspaper sitting on the table, and now it was all wet. Which made it harder to read it. But I got most of it.

It said LOCAL MAN JAILED ON CHILD ENDANGERMENT CHARGES.

I don't remember the whole thing word for word, but basically it said that Roger Manson had pleaded guilty and gone straight to county jail for ninety days, because if he'd gone to a trial, they would have tried to charge him with a lot more than that. Maybe even involuntary manslaughter. It was a plea bargain.

It also said that he'd made things worse by being drunk when the sheriff found him. That made it two different kinds of child endangerment, because even if the fishing trip had come off without a hitch, he was still clearly planning to drive us home in that condition. It said his blood alcohol was almost twice the legal limit. It didn't say he had almost five hours of drinking left to go. But I knew. Only, maybe he was planning to sober up by then? It didn't matter. This is how it all came down. If his intentions were any better, the world would never know.

And he was already in jail. Right now. And Will hadn't said a word. I couldn't believe it. He never mentioned his dad was in jail right now. Or who was at his house, taking care of him. Or if he was there all alone.

Another good reason to worry about Will.

When I got to school, I found Will at his locker.

"Hey," I said.

I tried to say it really normal. Like nothing could possibly be wrong. But I guess I failed miserably, because he said, "Yeah, I know, you read the paper. You and everybody else on the planet. So now you know. Apparently this is my fault, too."

"I never said that!"

"Not you. I know better than to think that about you. I'm talking about my dad. He didn't say it, either. But I'm not stupid. I can see it on his face."

We started off walking down the hall together. Leading this long bubble of silence everywhere we walked. Maybe it was my imagination, but it sounded quieter than yesterday's silence. Is that even possible?

I said, "Is there anybody at home with you?"

"Yeah. My mom."

"*Your mom?*"

"Yeah. She drove up from L.A. to stay with me for ninety days. And then every weekend her new boyfriend is coming up. Starting tonight." He sighed. "Life in the Manson family."

I stopped walking. "Does that feel really bad?" I couldn't even imagine. "Is that just, like, the most awful thing possible?"

He stopped, too. Looked down at the textbook in his hand. Like he suddenly couldn't live one more minute without reading the title. "Well, it's not *good*." Then he looked up, but not at me. Past me. Over my shoulder. I turned around and saw he was looking at Lisa Muller. Standing by her locker, talking to another girl. "On the other hand, it might be better than these last couple of weeks with my dad." He never took his eyes off her when he said it. "I really had nowhere to go but up." His expression changed, in a weird way. Like he got lighter all of a sudden. "That's it," he said.

"That's what?"

"I'm going to talk to Lisa Muller. I'm going to say something to make her laugh. Right now. This is the day."

I knew a bad idea when I heard one. "Oh, dude. I don't know. Not today, okay? You're sitting in too much crap already. Don't do anything rash."

"But that's just it," he said. "Don't you see? That's why it's so perfect. I have nowhere to go but up. My life can't possibly get any worse."

"Oooh. Don't say that. Never say that. It's tempting fate."

But I wasn't swaying him. I could tell.

"I'm going in. Cover my back. I mean, stay close. Stay close enough to see her smile. I want a witness."

I was holding his jacket sleeve. Trying to keep him from his doom. "What are you going to say?"

"I have no idea. I'm trusting fate. The first thing out of my mouth will have to be the right thing."

"This is a really half-baked plan, Will. I'm begging you. Sleep on this."

"No, this is it. I have nowhere to go but up."

He pulled his arm away from me and charged in, and I followed about five steps behind. He came up behind Lisa, so she didn't even have a chance of seeing him standing there. The girl Lisa was talking to saw him, though, and pointed. Not in a nice way. More like telling Lisa, *You* deal with this. Lisa turned around.

"Hello," Will said. And gave a little wave. Like he was the grand marshal of a parade or something.

My heart fell right down into my sneakers. My stomach went with it. This couldn't go anywhere from here except wrong.

"Uh . . . *yes?*" she said. Also not nice. Lots of bad stuff to read between the lines. Like, Why are you cursing me with your presence? And, You're already irritating me, so the rest of this better be good.

Now, Will is not a stupid guy. So he caught that. And it hurt his game. If he even had one. It tripped him up big-time. I knew the next words out of his mouth would be disastrous. But I was wrong. There were no next words. He just froze. Nothing came out.

"Yeah?" Lisa snapped. "What?"

That was not designed to help. And it didn't. Poor Will just kept standing there. Mute. Dying. See, I knew he was wrong. Never say it can't get worse. It can always get worse. On that note, one of the jocks came over and stood next to Lisa and put his arm around her.

"I have to go," she said. As she walked away, she turned to her jock boyfriend and made a comment. Maybe we weren't supposed to hear it. Maybe she was trying to be quiet. But she could have tried harder. Because I was five steps behind Will, and I heard it loud and clear. She said, "What a loser."

We both just stood there for the longest time. The hall emptied out, and then the bell rang. So there we were, out in the hall together, officially late for class. And I still didn't want to go up to him, or talk to him. I thought he might break if I touched him. I should've worked harder to talk him out of this. I should've tried harder. I think I let Will down.

After another tough minute or so, I went up and clapped him on the back. Gently. Just in case. "What a witch. Sorry. I know you wanted her to turn out to be nice."

Will's face wasn't what I expected. Just kind of still, like it was chiseled in stone. Not even pained-looking. Just empty and still. "No, she's right," he said. "She's absolutely right. I am a loser."

"Stop it. I won't let you do this."

"No, it's okay. Really. It's okay. It's better this way. It's better not to fight it. I'm a loser."

"Okay, we're going to pop you out of this, dude. I know, it's hard, but we'll be laughing about this in a few days." Honestly, I figured it would take a lot more than a few days, though. A thing like that, at a time like that, maybe months. Maybe years. But sooner or later I figured we'd laugh about it. I hoped. "Tell you what—after school we'll go by Grey's Café and get a couple of those Mount Everest–size banana splits. Good for what ails you."

He looked right into my eyes for the first time, and I

was shocked by what I saw there. It reminded me of the lingcod, coming at me with all those teeth. "That is *not* how I solve things," he said, nearly yelling. "That's how *you* solve things!"

I took a step back. More than a little bit stung. I guess it always comes out sooner or later. You think you can trust somebody, you think they're not like everybody else. But people are people, and if you give them enough rope, sooner or later they'll hang you.

"I'll see you later," I said.

About twenty steps down the hall I realized he was right behind me. I felt his hand on my shoulder.

"Stop," he said. "I'm sorry." But I didn't stop. "Please!" He yelled it. So loud a teacher stuck her head out into the hall to see what was going on. Then she disappeared again.

I turned and looked at him, and he looked so pathetic. So I held still and let him talk to me.

"I'm sorry," he said. "Really. I didn't mean to take it out on you. You're the last person who deserves that. Can we start over? Please? Let's try it your way. Really. Let's go out after school and try the sundae. I mean, who am I to knock it if I haven't tried it? It could help."

I sat on that for a minute, and then I nodded. I guess if you're really a friend, you overlook certain things. It's easy to be friends with someone who only says things you want to hear. I guess if you're really a friend, you have to cut a friend some slack.

*   *   *

We were about five bites into that mountain of bliss that is a Grey's Café sundae when I looked up and saw the two jocks come in. I knew right away it was no coincidence. They were here because we were. One of them was the boyfriend. Lisa's boyfriend. I think his name is Rusty. And he was with that other guy who's either the Mike or the Dave. This was all coming together in my head. Shaping up bad.

We were sitting at the counter, and they came over and stood right behind us. One of them pinched the fat on my sides. I'm ticklish, so I jumped a mile.

"Nice to see you finally eating something," he said. "You need the calories."

The waitress behind the counter looked up and frowned. "If you're here to eat, sit down and order. If not, get lost."

I felt them move away from behind us. Heard chairs scrape on the linoleum.

I gave the waitress a little thank-you smile, and she shook her head in disgust. At them, not at me. She was about fifty, and looked like she'd seen it all, and according to her name tag, her name was Angie.

"Hey, Charles," Rusty called out from his table. "You were very smooth today. I had no idea you had such a way with words."

I saw Will's eyes close. He put down his long spoon.

"Oooh, be careful," Mike/Dave said. "Don't piss him off."

"Why? What's he gonna do to me?"

"You really piss him off, he might take you fishing."

So there it was. The grace period was over. Silence gave way, and behind it was all the usual garbage. Made the silence look better all the time.

Angie said, "That's it. Out." She grabbed up the sign from behind the register that said WE RESERVE THE RIGHT TO REFUSE SERVICE TO ANYONE. Took it over to their table and held it right in their faces.

Which, you know, looking back on it . . . It goes to that thing about small towns. Because for her to react the way she did to a simple comment about fishing . . . I didn't see it at the time, but looking back, she must have known exactly who Will was and what had happened to his brother. No wonder he was having such a hard time.

"Hey, lady," Rusty said, "we weren't doing anything. Just talking to our friends over there."

Angie turned in the direction of the kitchen and cupped one hand beside her mouth. "Ralph!" She really bellowed it out. "We got trouble up here!"

Not three seconds later Ralph came banging through the swinging kitchen door. A big guy with a potbelly. Holding a cast-iron skillet. The jocks made it out the door in about half the time it would've taken Ralph to get over to their table.

I looked over at Will. He wasn't eating his sundae. I

went back to eating mine, because I didn't want it to melt. I didn't want to waste it.

"Thank you," he said. I thought he meant me. And I hadn't done anything. Then I realized he was talking to Angie and Ralph.

"Sure thing, honey," Angie said.

I ate seven or eight more bites of sundae.

I said, "I'm sorry, Will. I guess this was a bad idea. I guess a good idea would have been more like, buy a gallon of Häagen-Dazs and eat it at my house." Silence. Long silence. "But seriously, eat your sundae, dude. It's a total waste if it melts. Don't let them do that to you."

More silence. Then he slid his sundae over in front of me.

That was a tall order. Even for me. But I couldn't stand to think of all that good food going to waste. So I gave it my best shot.

I walked him all the way to the corner of his street. Finding lots of reasons to look over my shoulder. But they were never back there. I was surprised. I was fully prepared for the onslaught. But they were never there.

Meanwhile, I was trying to talk him into coming over to my house. "Wouldn't it be so much better than being home with your mom's new boyfriend?"

"They'll be gone," he said. "They have a date."

"You're kidding me."

"A thing like that I couldn't make up. Seems romance is very important. Especially now that they're forced to spend so much time sleeping apart."

"They actually *said* that to you?"

"Oh, yes indeed. I am in hell, all right. Yes, she said that. But what she didn't say is that she can't stand being in our house. Every time she passes Sam's room, she bursts into tears. But she refuses to talk about that. She won't even say his name. She just makes up a million excuses to be out."

"You should still come over. You shouldn't be alone."

"It'll be nice to be alone. Let it go, Ernie. I'm fine. It's all over now. Everything is fine."

By now we were almost at his corner.

"What do you mean it's all over now?"

"Just a figure of speech," he said. Walking away.

"Will? Are you going to be okay?"

He waved without turning around. He never answered me.

I was almost all the way home when something truly bizarre happened. The hood of my sweatshirt got caught on something, and it stopped me in my tracks, yanked my head backward, and made me choke, all at the same time.

I think it should be obvious that hoods don't catch on anything as you're walking down the middle of a sidewalk.

Your hood stays behind you. So if you don't snag on anything—and why would you?—neither should your hood.

Maybe that part went without saying. But you never know.

It all got a tiny bit clearer when I heard a jock voice from a few paces behind me.

Rusty said, "Hey, I hooked a big one!"

"Whoa! Think you can land that one? That looks like a giant blubberfish to me." Mike/Dave.

I had no idea what was holding me. I didn't really want to know. Nobody was literally holding on to my hood. I knew that because their voices were too far away.

I decided to put Mike/Dave's question to the test. I was a big fish. Maybe I could break the line and get away.

I kept moving. In the direction I'd been pointing to begin with. And I pulled hard. But I wasn't moving fast, I couldn't breathe, and it was beginning to freak me out.

Rusty kept yelling, "Get the net, Davey. Get the net!" Which didn't help.

I reached around and felt for the "line." Grabbed it and pulled it forward so I could really see it. Plain white twine. Definitely too strong to break. Then I grabbed hold of the hood and wrenched it around so I could see what they actually had me by. It was a real fishhook. A treble hook with a lure attached. And one of the three hooks had gone clean through my sweatshirt hood. And I knew it wasn't going to be easy to get it out again. They have barbs to keep them in place. So just unhooking it from my hood was not an option. I'd need to cut through the metal of the hook to get it out again.

I yanked hard, but no give. I yanked again. Just at that same moment, an old lady ran across the street, yelling, "What are you doing? What are you doing to that poor boy?" Unfortunately, that was the moment they dropped the "rod" and ran. So I yanked, expecting all this resistance, but there was nobody left to resist. My handful of string just came flying forward, and my hood came with it, and I felt a sharp pain in the back of my scalp. Because a fishhook had just lodged there. Now, apparently, I had one hook in my hood and another in me.

Great.

The old lady caught up to me as I was trying to feel how to get it out again.

"Oh, dear," she said. "What awful boys. Why would anyone do such an awful thing?"

I said, "I only hope that's the worst thing they ever do." Sounding more casual than I felt. Inside, where it counts, I was shook. "Can you just pull it out? I mean, from my head." As I said before, getting it out of my hood would be trickier.

"Oh, dear. I can't see around your sweatshirt hood. Let me move your hood."

She pulled on it slightly, and I yelled out loud. "Ow!

No. Don't move the hood. It still has a hook through it. We're stuck together."

"I can't even see what I'm doing. And I'm afraid it's going to bleed if I just pull."

Tell me. It's not like I never stuck myself with a fish-hook before. They don't like to go backward. They're built to resist the reverse gear. If they hook all the way through the skin, you're better off to cut the barb end with a wire cutter. Because it will definitely tear flesh otherwise. But if it's just sticking in there, you really have no choice.

"It has to come out," I said. "Here. I'll do it myself."

And I angled the barb as best I could and pulled hard. Swallowed the scream so as not to freak the poor old lady.

"Oh, dear," she said, peering at the back of my head. "It's bleeding a lot. Here, let me get you a tissue." She rummaged in her purse and handed me a clean pink tissue folded into quarters.

"Thanks," I said, and dabbed at the spot. Then I looked at the tissue. Alarmingly bloody.

On the sidewalk at my feet lay a plain stick with a three- or four-foot length of twine tied on. I picked it up and pulled the string off the end. Then I wrenched my hood around and examined it more closely. An old rusty minnow lure with three hooks. One bloody. Another still stuck in the fabric. Just my luck. They thought fishing was dorky, but they knew where to get their hands on a hook. I wondered if I'd ever know where it came from. Then again, did I really want to?

I walked the rest of the way home. Using the pink tissue to stall the bleeding from the back of my head. Trying to remember when I'd last had a tetanus shot. Trailing the length of string from the fishhook, still lodged in the back of my sweatshirt hood.

Did I mention that it was not a great day?

I stopped in the garage first and got down my tackle box. Pulled off my sweatshirt— *very* carefully—and cut the hook with my wire cutters. Threw the two pieces of hook and the string in the outside trash before going inside.

When I got in the house, my mother was in the kitchen, cooking.

I stuck my head in. I was careful to face her at all times so she wouldn't see the blood on the back of my hair. I couldn't hold pressure to it while she was watching. I could feel a trickle of blood roll down my neck.

"I'm making you a surprise," she said. "A special treat."

I thought, Okay, what's the most fattening thing you can possibly think of?

She said, "Homemade macaroni and cheese."

Yeah. That should do it. She makes the sauce with extra-rich milk. And about a pound and a half of cheddar cheese. No exaggeration. Then tops it all off with heavily buttered bread crumbs. But it really is fabulous. And I couldn't bring myself to tell her. Not now. It was a surprise for me. A special treat. Only the cruelest son in the world would tell her now.

I had no idea how I was going to eat any of it after my one and three-quarters banana splits. But somehow, for her, I knew I'd manage.

"It smells wonderful," I said.

Then I went into her bedroom and snuck her little hand mirror off the dresser, and took it in my bathroom and used it to look at the back of my head in the bathroom mirror. I kept pressing, but it didn't want to stop bleeding on its own.

I had done a bad job pulling out the hook. I forgot the part where you calm yourself and do it carefully. Do it right. I'd really ripped my scalp doing it in a panic.

I would have to hold pressure on it till it stopped bleeding, then wash the blood out of my hair and hope that didn't start it up all over again.

All before dinner.

While I was waiting I thought about Will and how glad I was that he got home safe before this happened. Better me than Will. Especially today. I'm not sure Will could take it today. I'm not sure his poor back would hold one more straw.

About seven o'clock I was doing some research online, for my history homework, and I got the jingle. It was

Will. Of course it was Will. Who else would instant-message me? Unless, of course, they were delivering a death threat.

i just want to say youve been a good friend ernie i just wanted to thank you for being my friend

I know that sounds like a nice thing to say. But it scared me. Just the fact that he would get sappy like that. I wrote him back right away.

DONT TALK LIKE ITS THE END OF THE WORLD

no its fine everything is fine now

SERIOUSLY DUDE ARE YOU OKAY YOU DONT SOUND OKAY

ive never been better everything is okay now

YOU SURE YOU DONT WANT TO COME OVER

yeah

WANT TO DO SOMETHING
TOMORROW

goodbye ernie thanks for
being my friend

WAIT WAIT DONT GO AWAY
WHAT DO YOU MEAN GOODBYE

I waited. No answer. I rang him back. Nothing. Then I
saw his little symbol disappear off my messenger list. He'd
gone off-line.

I grabbed up the phone and called him. No answer.

Now, what do you do in a situation like that? What the
hell kind of position does that put me in? Was I supposed
to run over there and see if he was okay? I would have, in a
heartbeat. But I knew he probably wouldn't answer the
door if he wouldn't answer the phone. So what good would
that do?

Or was I supposed to call 911 and tell them we might
have an actual emergency on our hands here? And then,
what if I was wrong? What if all these ambulances and police cars went screaming over there, and they broke down
his door with an ax or something, and it turned out he was
just in there trying to be alone? But if you're just home

trying to be alone, why message your best friend and say goodbye? That led me to an even worse question. What if I was right? What if no police cars or ambulances went screaming over and we really did have an emergency on our hands?

I picked up the phone and called 911.

The dispatcher lady kept trying to get me to calm down and give her really specific information. I guess I was trying to explain too much about his message, and his awful day, and other stuff she couldn't really work with. So I gave her his address.

But she kept saying, "What is the nature of the emergency?"

I got more direct and said he might try to do something stupid. Clearly that was not direct enough.

She said it again. "What exactly is the nature of the emergency?"

I realized I was trying every way in the world to keep from saying it. And I had to stop that now. It was the truth, and I had to spit it out. I had to be a man and face those really harsh words.

I said, "I think he might try to kill himself."

"So you're saying there's a possible suicide in progress at this address?"

"Yes."

"We'll get an emergency response team right over there."

I hung up the phone and just sat there. I felt like I

couldn't move. Like I was paralyzed. I was thinking, What did I just do?

I couldn't possibly bring myself to wish I was right. Of course I didn't wish that. But what a mess if I was wrong! I was in this weird situation where it was impossible to hope for the best. It was almost like there was no best to hope for.

It was just a bad night no matter how you slice it.

When I could move again, I got up and found my mom in the kitchen. Cleaning up the dishes. Also polishing off the leftovers.

"I'm going over to Will's," I said.

"On a school night?"

"It's Friday."

"Oh, that's right. So it is. T.G.I.F."

"Thanks," I said, and got out as fast as I could. Or tried to anyway.

"Ernie, wait." I froze, wondering what now. "You have blood on the back of your hair."

Great. Just great. Good moment for that, all right. All that washing. Twice. And it still had to bleed a little more. Just enough so my mom could bust me.

"Oh. That. Right. It was stupid. I stuck myself with a fishhook. I was practicing casting."

I turned around to look, to see how the lie was going over.

"Practicing casting?"

"Right."

"But you're the best at casting."

"Oh. Well. Sure. Because I practice." She opened her mouth to speak, but I cut her off. "Can we talk when I get home from Will's?"

"Sure. I guess. Sure, honey. You want a ride over there?"

That was a good question. Did I? It would be faster. But then my mom would see the ambulance. She'd freak out. And she wouldn't just drop me there. She'd be with me through the whole fiasco. I love my mom, but she's not so good in a crisis. I'd be spending the whole time keeping her calm.

"No, that's okay. Thanks. I'll walk. It's good for me."

I ran out before she could answer.

When I got to Will's house, I was so out of breath I was worried I might be about to have a heart attack. And I wasn't running, either. Just walking as fast as I could. I mean, as fast as I could without dying.

There was a police car there, and an ambulance in his driveway.

One of the cops was talking to the two EMT guys. It didn't look like they were doing very much. It didn't look like enough.

I went right up to the other cop. The one who was still standing by the squad car.

"I'm the one who called 911," I said. "Will's my best friend."

"Is he in there alone?"

"Yeah, his mom and her boyfriend are out for the evening."

"We're going to have to break down the door."

I got this sudden cramp in the pit of my stomach. What if Will had clicked off-line and then walked out the door? What if he wasn't answering the phone or the door because he wasn't even home? What if this was all a terrible mistake?

But he said goodbye. Why would he say goodbye?

"What if I'm wrong?" I asked the cop. "What if you break down their door and I'm wrong?"

"What if we don't break down the door and you're right?"

"Right," I said. "You better break down the door."

The two cops got this battering ram out of the trunk of their car. It wasn't what I expected. It wasn't big and impressive, like in those old movies where somebody storms a castle with a battering ram that's like the trunk of a giant tree. It was just this iron thing about a foot and a half long, or maybe two feet, I don't know, with a handle on each side. The cops each took one handle and carried it up to Will's front door. The whole inside of me felt numb and cold, like it was floating in a freezing ocean. They swung it back, then hit Will's front door once. It broke open, but it didn't swing wide, because the security chain stopped it.

That's when I felt something in all that numbness. Something like a little electric shock. Because you can't go out and put the chain on behind you. If the chain is on, you're home.

They hit it again, and the door swung wide, and long splinters of wood flew around at the end of the chain.

The EMTs went running in.

We waited. And waited.

"Do I have to wait here?" I asked the cops.

One of them said, "No, you can go home now, son."

That was *so* not what I meant.

"I mean can I go in and see if he's okay?"

"Oh. No. Let the EMTs do their job. You wait out here with us."

So I waited. And waited. And waited.

Then they came back out with Will on a stretcher. And I didn't feel anything inside. I don't mean I didn't care. I just mean it was all dead in there. Whatever there was to feel, I couldn't feel it. Yet.

"Is he okay?" I yelled out.

"He's still with us," one of the EMTs yelled back.

"I need to go with him," I told the cops. "Can I go to the hospital with him? I'm his best friend."

"I think that's just for blood family," he said.

So I just stood there on the lawn until long after the

ambulance roared away with the siren screaming. Then I got tired of standing, so I sat on the lawn. Long after the cops finished their report and drove away.

Then I got up and closed the front door so they wouldn't get robbed, and so Sampson wouldn't get out. I had no idea where Sampson was. I had no idea why he didn't bark during any of this. But he was in there some-where. And I didn't want him wandering off after I left.

Then I walked home.

My mom drove me to the hospital.

She didn't say much. Thank God. She was pretty much silent all the way there. But she frowned the whole time. And I had a bad feeling I knew what she was thinking. And that it was something along the lines of, Maybe you shouldn't be friends with this Will boy if it's always going to be some disaster like this.

Like, yeah, just what he needs. To have his only friend give up on him.

I said something I was proud of myself for saying. I said, "I need you to just drop me there."

"Why shouldn't I come in?"

"I need you to go over to Will's house and wait for his mother. Somebody has to tell his mother why the door is broken and Will is gone. Somebody has to tell her he's at Twin Cities." Then, this is the part I was proud of. "Besides. This is something I need to do by myself."

She frowned even harder. "I just worry that since you've been friends with Will . . . I worry that you're learning *too* much about life."

"How can I learn too much about life? Besides, what would Uncle Max say?"

"I don't know. What would he say?"

"He'd say you don't have to keep telling me what to be afraid of, because I already know. He'd say I've had a trauma and I need you to support me now. Take care of my insides."

She just sighed.

Then we pulled up in front of the emergency room, and I said thanks for the ride and jumped out. And, amazingly, she did what I asked her to do. She drove away.

I kept asking the woman at the admitting desk about Will. Three or four times. She just kept saying a doctor would come out and talk to me as soon as he could.

I sat on this hard plastic chair in the waiting room until I finally saw somebody coming. He was an Indian guy. From India, I mean. Pretty young, but already a little bald. Really short and really skinny. Less than half of me. Size-wise, I mean.

"Is Will okay?" I asked before he even got down the hall to me.

"It looks good," he said.

I breathed in a way I hadn't breathed all night.

He stopped right in front of me. "Where are the parents?"

"Well, his dad's in jail. And his mom is out with her boyfriend on a date and she doesn't even know this happened. But my mom's at his house, so when they get back, she'll tell them. So, he's going to be okay?"

"Looks that way. The pills hadn't been in his system long. We pumped his stomach and probably got most of it. I doubt there was ever a lethal dose in his bloodstream."

"So when can he come home?"

"Minimum three days."

"But you said he was okay."

He just stood there a minute. Like he wished he didn't have to say what he was about to say next. "Case like this, I have no choice but to order a 5150." I think it was clear by the look on my face that I had no idea what he was talking about. "Three-day mandatory psychiatric evaluation."

"Oh."

It sounded kind of awful. But then again, Will probably needed that. He needed somebody to see that he was dying inside. Maybe it would be a good thing. Maybe they'd really get him some kind of help.

"Are you the one who called this in?" he asked.

"Yeah. That was me."

"Well, you probably saved his life. Because if he'd been home alone all evening, I wouldn't like his chances one bit. If you hadn't called it in, he probably wouldn't be here right now. Have the receiving desk call me when his mother gets here, okay?"

I went back to that hard plastic chair and sat down. The room was so bright, and I was tired, and the bright was starting to hurt my eyes and the inside of my head. I looked at the giant clock on the wall. It was a little after ten. I knew it might be hours before I got a ride home. And I was so tired. I just wanted to go to bed.

I wanted to write all this in my diary and then sleep for a decade.

I closed my eyes to try to keep the bright out. But it was even a little bright through my eyelids. I opened my eyes, and the woman at the admitting desk smiled at me. That's when I broke down and cried. It didn't matter that I hated to cry in front of anybody. It didn't make any difference. There was nothing I could do. It was like a flash flood. Like a dam giving up under pressure. I couldn't have stopped it if I'd tried.

And, actually, I didn't try.

December 1st

When I went back to school this morning, that whole miserable feeling thing came up all over again. Only this time I didn't cry. I mean, I was in school. I'm not stupid. I know what to keep to myself and when. Especially when I'm down behind enemy lines.

First period I sit three seats behind Lisa Muller. Three behind and one over. I found myself staring at her a lot. Somehow she must have felt me staring, because every now and then she'd look over her shoulder at me. I could tell it was making her uncomfortable.

And, you know what? I didn't care. Her comfort wasn't high on my list. Way I see it, some people are too comfortable as it is.

I know she knew about Will. Everybody knew. It was all over town, and I don't really know how. But that's a small town for you. It has its own private public-address system. You just start with anybody, and then it's like a snowball rolling downhill.

After class I followed her all the way to her locker. I don't know what came over me, but I was mad. Which is weird, because I never get mad. It just isn't in me. Or if it's in there somewhere, I guess I don't feel it. But I felt it today.

She opened her locker like there was nothing wrong. Like I wasn't standing right there staring at her.

Then all of a sudden she spun around and started yelling at me. Really went ballistic. "What? What do you want? Why do you keep looking at me? I didn't do anything. What?"

I didn't answer for a minute. Just watched her fall apart. I was thinking, I've never been in a situation like this, where I'm in a confrontation with somebody and they aren't the one holding all the cards.

I said, "I just want to know what you tell yourself in your head at a time like that." And it was true. I wanted to know. I had to know. My curiosity had reached the breaking point. This was a mystery of human nature I needed to solve. "I mean, when you say something like that to somebody, what do you tell yourself in your head to justify it?"

"I didn't say anything to him!"

"Oh, come on. If you say it loud enough for him to hear it, you're saying it to him."

"You better not be trying to blame me for what he did. Because he had lots of other reasons. His brother dying. And his father going to jail and all."

I nodded. Weirdly calm. It was like a side of me I wasn't used to seeing. "Interesting," I said. "It's interesting that you knew all that about his life, you knew he was going through all that, but you still chose that moment to dump one more thing on him. I'm not trying to hang you out to dry, I'm really not. I'm serious. I just really want to know what happens in your head that lets you justify treating somebody that way."

She never told me.

Instead she turned around, slammed her locker door hard. Her hair flying all around. When she turned back, I saw she was crying. Then she ran away down the hall.

That did not go well, I thought to myself. And when I thought it, I realized how much I missed Will. Because normally, he would be right by my side or right behind me at a time like this. And I could turn to him and say, That did not go well. And somehow that would take the edge off. Make it a little easier to swallow.

I said it out loud anyway. To myself. "That did not go well." Then I went on to my next class.

I was on my way down the stairs from lunch when I saw the four jocks on the landing. I stopped, knowing trouble when I saw it. Just stopped and let this sea of bodies swarm past me. Then I thought, Maybe this is a tactical error. Maybe I'm making a terrible mistake to let the bulk of the student body thin out before I face them. Safety in numbers and all that. So I decided I would try to pass by. But I had frozen just long enough that I was the last one down the stairs. Great.

But there was no safety in those numbers anyway, and part of me knew it. None of those kids was about to go to bat for me. Alex had gone by, looking uncomfortable. But there was nothing he could do, so he looked away. Professional courtesy ends here.

Just as I was stepping down onto the landing, I heard Rusty say, "Oh, look. It's the fat boy who blamed *my* girlfriend because *his* friend is a lunatic and a freak."

See what I mean about how fast word travels in a small town? But I shouldn't joke. I sure was in no mood to joke while it was happening.

Now, here's what turned out to be my fatal mistake: I didn't look down.

Basic safety says you look for the foot. The foot they inevitably stick out to trip you. It's kind of an obvious one. Not really hard to see it coming.

It's not even that I forgot. I didn't, exactly. It's more like the reason I don't glance nervously over my shoulder as I walk down the hall. Like that sense that if you act like you see it coming, that's worse. And yet, if you hear their footsteps barreling down on you from behind, it might pay you to look around.

I really screwed up big-time.

I tried to walk by like nothing was wrong. Didn't look in their eyes. Didn't look at their feet. Next thing I knew, I was flying forward, scrambling to get my balance back. But with all that weight balanced forward, I kept going. Forward.

Now, the place where they tripped me was pretty far from the stairs. On the landing, but not near the edge of it. The last thing I want to do is make excuses for them. But really, I might as well face it. This was an issue of my size.

If it had been one of them, they would have either fallen on their face or gotten their balance back. But either way, they would have done it on the safety of the landing.

But it was me.

And once my weight got thrown forward like that, it was impossible for me to stop. And then there was the edge of the stairs, and I was still flying. So I flew down the stairs. Or down quite a few of them anyway. And when I landed, I landed hard.

I didn't make it all the way to the floor below. I guess that's good. I guess it's good that I belly flopped, too. I'd hate to think what would've happened if I'd landed headfirst. Could've broken my neck or something. But that was the only good news. Everything else was pretty bad. It knocked the wind out of me and bruised my chin and three places along my ribs where I caught the edges of steps. And I banged up my knees. But I stayed there, thank God. Didn't roll down. I guess that's another bit of good news. You need all the good news you can get on a day like this.

I heard Rusty say, "Oh, shit!"

Another one of them said, "Great idea, asswipe." But I couldn't tell which one.

Then a jumble of their voices, impossible to tell apart.

"He wasn't supposed to fall down the stairs."

"What if he broke his neck?"

"This wasn't my idea anyway."

"See if he's okay."

"Not me. I don't want to!"

"Well, somebody has to see if he's okay."

A minute later I felt someone lean over me. I was holding still. Trying to breathe. Still trying to get some air into my lungs. I could actually feel his breath on the back of my neck, he was that close.

"Hey. Are you okay?"

I wanted to say something clever. Like, Depends on your definition of the word okay. But what came out was more like a grunt.

"I think he's okay!"

A thunder of footsteps as they all ran past me and into the hall below.

"Wait," I heard one of them say. Sounded like Rusty. "We have to make sure he gets up."

"I'm getting out of here. This was all *your* idea. *You* make sure he gets up."

Another difficult second or two. Then I raised my head.

I looked down the hall, and there was Rusty. All by himself. His so-called buddies had run off and left him to face this alone.

I looked into his eyes. He was deeply, genuinely scared.

It was a weird moment for me. Because it made him seem so . . . almost . . . human. Like he was used to being in control but suddenly everything was totally out of control. And I could see how unprepared he was for this unexpected turn of events.

But, fear and all, he was going to wait there. To make sure I had survived.

I could breathe by then. More or less. So I said, "I'm pretty much alive."

And he took off running.

It took me a minute to get up. Everything hurt. I was saying to myself, I will not cry. I will not cry. I won't do it. It was hard, but I just refused. I just wasn't going to let a thing like that happen at a time like this.

I looked up to see a couple of girls watching from the end of the hall, but when they saw me looking, they quick turned and walked away.

For a minute I just stood there, trying to get back into my own head again. Trying to be okay.

It hit me all of a sudden. Right. I remember now. That's why I don't get mad. That's why I don't confront them. I'd forgotten. But how could I have forgotten? How can you forget something you know so well? I figured it had to do with getting mad. So I decided, That's it. No more of this feeling crap. It's bad for my health.

I started to limp off to my next class, but then I thought, No. That's enough. I don't have to take a thing like that and go on like nothing ever happened. This was getting to be too much.

Instead I went into the nurse's office and told her I tripped and fell down the stairs. Which was more or less true. Not exactly the truth, the whole truth, and nothing but the truth. But not exactly a lie, either. Okay, I got tripped. Didn't exactly do it on my own. Then again, when someone trips you, you trip. Right? Okay. Enough playing with words. I said what I said, and I would have to live with it.

She called my mother, and my mother left work early to come get me.

I couldn't just keep walking through some crap like this, like it never happened. Like everything was fine.

Every now and then you need to call a time-out. Get your breath back.

December 2nd

This morning I woke up with a bad feeling in the pit of my stomach. I knew I'd crossed some kind of line. Worse yet, I knew I'd never get back to the old side again.

The problem was a sticky one. I didn't want to go back to school. I didn't want to do it anymore. Ever. Not that I had any good alternatives. There's only one high school in this town. But that awful thing sitting in my stomach was like a stubborn little kid. It just said no. The logic didn't matter. There's no reasoning with a feeling.

I didn't want to keep doing it.

My mother came in early to see how I was.

"Do I have to go to school today?"

"Well, no, honey, not if you're really sore."

"I am."

"Okay, well, if you get up and come to the table, I'll make French toast before I go to work. Are you okay here all by yourself today?"

"Mom. I'm not a baby."

"Right. Of course you're not."

She hurried out of my room, and I decided French toast was worth getting up for. But I had no idea how hard it was going to be to get up.

My ribs were just killing me. The whole middle part of my body, actually. Also my knees. And my neck was really sore, I guess from the shock it took when I hit my chin. And my arms were really sore, because I guess without even realizing it I put my arms out to try to catch myself. I could feel it all the way up through my shoulders. It even hurt to breathe all the way in.

I felt like I'd been hit by a bus. Seriously.

But I knew if I couldn't get up, my mom would rush me to the hospital or something. And I didn't think I needed a hospital. It wasn't that bad. It just hurt. I was just sore all over.

I had to use my arms to lift my head, but it was hard to lift my arms. But when I got my head up, I could sit up. Then I just sat there for a minute before I tried to get up. Actually, standing up wasn't really that bad.

I tried to put a robe on over my pajamas, but it hurt so

much to try to get my arms into it that I just gave up and
dropped it on the floor. I wasn't that cold anyway.

Home alone is a nice thing. I get it now, why Will said
that. Why he said it would be good to be alone. When
you're alone, you're safe. Plus you don't have to pretend to
anyone. You can just be yourself, not put on a good face.

I think that's why Will's my best friend. Because I
know I'm safe with Will and I don't need to pretend about
anything. I don't need to act like it's all okay. He knows
better, anyway.

About a minute after I thought that, the phone rang.

It was Will.

"Are you home?" I asked. Like I couldn't believe it.

"Yeah."

"And you don't have to go to school?"

"Not till I'm ready."

"How did you know I'd be home?"

"I didn't. I just thought I was going to leave a message
on your machine. Why are you home? Are you sick?"

"Not really."

"Then why are you home?"

"Long story," I said. "If I could, I'd come over and visit
you. But I don't think I'm up to that."

"I'll come visit *you*."

"Your mom doesn't care? She doesn't want you to
stay home?"

"My mom could care less what I do. If I just stay out of her face and never once say the word Sam, she's happy. Give me fifteen minutes," he said, and hung up the phone. Just like that.

I got up and unlocked the door, because it wouldn't pay to try to do a thing like that on short notice.

At first Will just stood there. Not saying anything. Just standing over my bed, looking like his body was in the room but the rest of him was somewhere else. He never looked in my eyes, but I saw him steal a glance at my chin. I hadn't looked at myself in the mirror yet. But I guess it must've looked bad.

"What did they do to you? And why?"

See? That's what I like about Will. No pretending.

"They tripped me, and I fell down the stairs."

"Did they bother to give you a reason? Or don't they even need one anymore?" He pulled up a chair. Pulled it over close to the bed, then sat down and peered into my face like he was noticing me for the first time. Like he'd just now seen me lying there.

"They didn't mean for me to go down the stairs."

"Okay. Assuming you're right, which I'm not sure of . . . did they bother to give you a reason why they tripped you?"

"It had something to do with my telling Lisa Muller she's a horrible person."

"You said that?"

"Not in so many words. But she seemed to take my meaning."

"So in other words, you were sticking up for me."

"Maybe. I guess. Yeah."

"Don't you know that only makes it worse?" He said it with this little teasing thing in his voice. Reminding me that I was the one who knew that. That I was the one who usually tried to tell it to him.

It hit me that I wanted to talk about what he did. And that we weren't talking about it. That we were talking all around it. And I wanted to change that, but I didn't know how to start.

So I just said, "Yeah. I don't really know where my head was with that. I kind of lost it. My head, I mean. I kind of lost my head."

I expected him to make some little toss-off comment about that, but instead he looked straight into my eyes and said, "Why didn't you just let me die?"

Then he got up and started walking around my room. Touching everything. The model airplanes flying from the ceiling. The frame around the picture of me with the eighteen-inch rainbow trout. Even things that have no real feel to them, like my autographed poster of Jerry Rice, from way back when he was still a 49er. Just walking around touching everything, and not looking at me.

"That is, like, the weirdest, dumbest question. I don't

even know what to say to a question like that. Why would I sit back and let my best friend die? Who would do a thing like that?"

"What if I *wanted* to die?" he asked, still not looking at me. Still touching. My fishing books. The top of the TV.

"You didn't." I said it with that same weird calm I remember from when I was losing my head and confronting Lisa Muller.

He looked at me for a split second, then quick looked away again. "How can you say that? You don't know that."

"Will. You messaged me and said goodbye. You practically told me what you were going to do before you did it."

"So I was supposed to die without even telling my best friend goodbye?"

"If you'd really wanted to die, you'd have written me a note thanking me for being your friend. You'd have written me a goodbye note. And then I would've gotten your message, but only later, when it would be too late." He didn't answer, even though I waited. What could he say? I was right, and we both knew it. "Look, it's not an insult. I mean, the part of you that wanted to be saved, that's a good thing. That's how we know you're marginally sane."

"I don't feel marginally sane," he said.

It got quiet after that.

I thought about school. And how I couldn't stay home forever.

"I told my mom I was too sore to go to school," I said.

Somebody had to say something. Somebody had to change the subject. At least somewhat. "Not entirely true."

He came back and sat on the chair beside the bed. Leaned his chin on his fists. "I don't want to go back there, Ernie. And I have no idea what to do about that."

It felt so good to hear him say that. It's so nice not to be the only person on the planet who knows how a thing like that feels.

"Yeah. I know. Believe me, I know. Me too. It's gotten really bad. It's gotten so much worse all of a sudden. It's like you almost get used to the insults. The verbal stuff. The fish imitations. I mean, you don't, but . . . you deal with it. You get to a point where you just deal with it. But then they turn up the heat on you. I mean, just since I last saw you there was the tripping incident and also they played a game where they tried to hook me like a fish and I ended up with the hook in the back of my scalp."

"Really? Where? Let me see."

I had to ask him to help me pick up my head, but then he parted my hair. Touched the little scab gently. Weirdly gentle. Didn't say anything, though.

"Don't say anything in front of my mom, because she doesn't know." I just stopped talking for a minute and listened to the silence, echoing around. Will set my head back down, really carefully. "You know that thing they call PTSD?" I asked.

He shook his head.

"Post-traumatic stress disorder?"

"Oh. Yeah."

"I feel like I've got something like current-traumatic stress disorder. Something that's not post. Mid-traumatic stress disorder. MTSD. How does that sound?"

"Like a city bus company or something. But I know what you mean."

"What are we going to do?"

"I don't know," he said. "But I'm going to do something. I'm going to do something about it. Something permanent. You don't deserve this crap. You don't deserve any of this. I'm going to find a way to put a stop to this once and for all."

I didn't ask what he meant. I figured he was just upset. I wasn't sure he meant anything by it, really. Maybe just blowing off steam. It's nice to talk from a power place, like you can do something. Whether it's true or not.

Neither one of us could seem to think of anything more to say, so Will turned on the TV and found a really bad soap opera. Sometimes we like to goof on weird stuff like that. It's just funny, even if it doesn't mean to be.

I wanted to ask him if he had to see a shrink now. I wanted to ask how this had changed things. What his life was going to be like from now on. But I didn't know how to bring it up. And I didn't know if he wanted me to. So I never did.

Besides, it was nice, anyway, just sitting there watching TV.

After about two hours of bad television Will said, "I miss fishing so much. I don't think I'll ever be able to bring myself to do it again. And I really hate that. Because I need it. It used to help me blow off steam somehow. We should go hunting."

"I don't know about that."

"Oh, come on, Ernie. It'd be good for you. You're too softhearted. You need to take command a little more. You'd like the way it makes you feel. And you eat meat, right? So what's the difference? I mean, if you get it from the store or shoot it yourself. It's still an animal."

"I know. I'm not saying it's wrong."

"So you'll go with me?"

"What about trout fishing?" I was hoping to change the subject. "You could bring yourself to do *that*, right?"

"I guess. I don't know."

"I might get to go up to my uncle Max's cabin for Christmas vacation. Maybe you could come."

"He won't let me."

"How do you know?"

"He won't. I know he won't. Nobody wants me around. Except you. Nobody likes trouble. And that's me. I'm trouble."

"Sometimes Uncle Max'll surprise you."

"If we get to go up there, will you try going hunting with me once?"

I think maybe you should be willing to try everything at least once, so I said, "Yeah, I guess."

After that we really didn't talk much again for the rest of the day. But it was nice, anyway, just sitting there with Will, watching TV. It was the best day in as long as I can remember. I wanted to do nothing but that for the rest of my life.

I went back to school today. Will and I both did. I hated it, but I did it. Because I'd already taken the whole week off. Plus the weekend. If I hadn't been better by this morning, my mom would've taken me to get my whole body x-rayed or something. And that's not fair. We can't really afford that, and I know I didn't break anything. I just didn't want to go back to school.

Will and I had the best week home. It was incredible. It was like a vacation from my whole life. My mom. School. Bullies. Going out into the world and seeing how people look at me. Everything. Escape from everything. It was heaven.

It was just me and Will, in my room, all week long.

We watched TV, played video games. We even played Monopoly once. And Scrabble three times. And he taught me how to play gin, and we played about a million games of that. One day he even brought some rented movies from the video store.

We ate peanut butter and jelly sandwiches until they were coming out of our ears, because it's something I knew how to fix for us.

Sometimes we talked, but nothing really earth-shattering.

Once I asked him if he was seeing a shrink, and he said yes and no. He said he was supposed to be, but he was blowing off the appointments, and so far nobody was calling him on it. His mom didn't care enough to check.

On Wednesday I called Uncle Max to ask if Will could come up for Christmas vacation. If my mom even let me go, that is.

"Yes," he said. Just like that.

"Wow," I said. "That's so cool of you. I thought maybe you'd mind because you said it should be just you and me."

He said, "Actually, what I meant is that you might need a vacation from your mom now and then. Is Will's mom going to let him go on Christmas?"

"I think she likes it better when he's not around. I think he makes her think about Sam."

Sure enough, after I was done talking to Uncle Max, Will called his mom and asked her. He looked a little unhappy, so I thought she might be saying no. I couldn't tell from his end of the conversation. All he really said was, "Uh-huh."

When he hung up the phone, he said, "She's thrilled. She just could not be more thrilled. Now she gets to go back down to L.A. for the holidays and not walk past Sam's old room anymore. She didn't say that but I know that's what she means. I've never heard her sound so happy."

"Great," I said. But I knew that was a mixed blessing for Will. She could have at least sounded like she cared about him. She could have pretended to care. She didn't even care that she didn't care. It was sad.

"Know what she said when I got home from the hospital?"

I shook my head. Of course I didn't know. But I knew it would be bad.

"She said, 'I needed those pills. Now what the hell am I supposed to do without my sleeping pills all month?'"

"That's it? That's all she said?"

"Oh. Well, no. That's not the *only* thing. She screamed and cried for about an hour and said I was the only son she had left and I had no right to take that away from her. How dare I try to take her only remaining son? And then when she was all cried out, she got this weirdly stony look on her face and said that thing about the pills."

I think I just said something like, "Wow."

Anyway, back to today.

Wait, no, I have to back up again. I'm sorry. I'm leaving important stuff out.

Thursday I told Will that I'd have to go back to school Monday morning. Otherwise my mom would start to freak.

"Okay," he said. "I'll go with you, so somebody has your back. You won't have to worry. I'll be covering your back."

"How?"

"Leave that up to me."

The next day he came over with this canister of pepper spray he'd stolen from his mother's purse.

I said, "Will, if we ever used that on them, it'd be all over. As soon as they could see again, they'd kill us."

"Me," he said. "They'll have to kill me. You won't be using it. You'll just be minding your own business. They'll have to come after me."

It seemed like a plan with some holes. Not to mention being a little . . . what am I trying to say? It's like when you say they're going to kill you, you don't mean they're going to *kill* you. And pepper spray seemed more like something you use on somebody who's actually going to kill you. It felt weird, like the whole issue was not exactly life or death except in Will's head. Like he took it and made it that way, and I couldn't stop him.

I felt like I was in the middle in this weird way that's hard to explain. I wasn't going to try to excuse those guys. Because they were plenty bad enough. But they weren't as bad as they were in Will's current brain. And I knew it.

Just not what to do about it.

But maybe it would make Will feel better to carry it. And it would never come out of his pocket if nothing went wrong.

Maybe I should have said something. But I didn't.

So, back to today. Today we went back to school.

Now, this was the first time any of those people had seen Will since he tried to kill himself. So it was like that silence thing all over again. But a little different this time. Not silent like pity, more silent like fear. Like they were afraid of him. Which I could immediately see was going to work on our side. I just didn't know how long it would last.

We never split up. When we had classes that weren't together, I'd be slow to get up and gather my books, and by the time I got out to the hall, there he would be. Waiting to walk me to my next class. We just stuck together, and everybody left us alone.

I still had really bad MTSD all day, but nothing happened.

When we were walking home at the end of school, Will said, "Did you notice something interesting? How respectful everybody was? See, that's the cool thing about carrying a weapon. You don't even need to use it. Just carrying it changes you. Gives you more confidence. And then people know to stay out of your way."

I had a very different theory. I figured they all had the Lisa Muller syndrome. Nobody wants to mistreat somebody and then find out he went home and tried to kill himself. It's too weird. It's like if Will had some kind of brittle-bone disease. Everybody would leave him alone so they wouldn't have to feel guilty when he shattered into a thousand pieces.

That was my theory, anyway. But I didn't share it with Will.

But maybe I should have.

But, first off, I could be wrong. Or maybe it was both things, I don't know. Plus why not be supportive? Why rain on his parade?

Besides, Will's confidence was a good thing. Will's confidence was my salvation. Well. My best shot at it, anyway. My best long shot.

I didn't bring my journal up to Uncle Max's cabin. I wanted to. I really did. And I missed having it there. There were a dozen times I'd have given my right arm to be able to write our whole day down. But I left it home, because of Will.

See, I'd promised Will I'd keep certain secrets. And I thought it might make him nervous if he knew everything was written down somewhere. Like somebody might find it and read it or something. So I just let the journal be *my* little secret.

But now I have to go back and try to remember everything that happened and write it all down. Before I forget it forever.

I'll start with the day we celebrated Christmas. It wasn't really Christmas, it was really Saturday the twentieth. The plan was that my mom would drive Will and me up to Uncle Max's house in Lemoore, and we'd all celebrate Christmas early, and then she'd go home and we'd drive up to the cabin the next day.

But there was a flaw in the plan. Will showed up empty-handed.

I don't mean he didn't have clothes and gear. He did. Two suitcases and plenty of outdoor wear and warm stuff. He even brought two of his dad's hunting rifles. And Sampson. Well, he had to bring Sampson. There'd be nobody home to take care of him. So he brought tons of stuff, but no presents. His mom hadn't even bothered to send him with any presents. Here we were driving up there to have an early Christmas dinner and open presents. And everybody would have presents to open but Will.

I pulled my mom aside and asked her about it. Before we left our house. She said she felt bad for him, but she couldn't really do anything about it, because she'd gotten me one big present instead of a few little ones. She asked if I had something I could give him, but I said Will and I had already agreed not to get presents for each other, because we really don't have much money, and the vacation together is kind of a giant present anyway.

So we just drove up there, still not knowing what we'd do. When we got to Uncle Max's house, he was making

Christmas dinner. Roast turkey with cranberry sauce and green beans and salad. And fresh fruit salad with chopped pecans sprinkled on top for dessert.

My mom walked around the kitchen and looked at everything. Like if she just looked hard enough, she would find where all the rest of the dinner was hiding.

"Well," she said. "That looks very . . . healthy."

You could tell she didn't get it, and Uncle Max shot me a bad look. He gave me this look that said, Oh, Ernie. You still haven't told her.

He was right. I still hadn't told her.

Right before dinner he pulled me aside into his den. I thought he was going to ream me out for not telling my mom I was trying to lose weight. Or wanting to lose weight, anyway. Not really doing so hot, but wanting to. But it was nothing about that.

He took two wrapped presents out of the big oak chest in the corner of his den. Set them down on his writing desk. We both stared at them like we expected them to do something.

"Lila tells me Will's mother didn't get him anything. And that's a problem, right? So let's just say for the sake of conversation that one of these presents is for Will." I picked one up and looked at the gift tag. It said, "To Ernie, from Uncle Max." I picked up the other one. It said, "To Ernie, from Uncle Max."

"Now, I hate to spoil Christmas surprises," Uncle Max

said, "but one of them is a collapsible ultralight rod and reel. The kind that telescopes down to almost nothing and you can put it right in your backpack. But it's not stiff, like most collapsibles. It's a real trout rod. Nice and sensitive. The other is a book on fly tying, with a kit to get someone started. Now, I hate to even ask this of you, but you're a young man now, and you can make tough decisions. Is one of these a present to Will from our family?"

"Yes," I said. "Absolutely. He should have the rod."

"You're sure."

The rod was the bigger, better present, and we both knew it.

"Yes. Positive. Will doesn't have an ultralight. I *have* one, at least. It doesn't break down, but at least I have one. And besides, I'll get something from Mom, too. I'm the one who wants to learn to fly-fish anyway. What good would that do Will? He hasn't even learned to trout-fish with bait yet. Will should get the rod." I felt like I was talking too much. Like I was trying to talk myself into it.

Uncle Max looked right into my face, and I had to look away, because I knew that look was a compliment, and compliments make me nervous. In my head I was begging him not to say anything nice out loud.

He must've heard me.

"So be it," he said. "Ernie has spoken."

"Thanks, though. For the collapsible rod. That was a really nice present."

I don't think Uncle Max likes compliments, either. All he said was, "Yeah, well. You know you're my favorite nephew."

My mom had about four helpings of turkey. She's not a big fan of anything green. She had two helpings of fruit salad, too. That was the only time she said anything about the dinner. She said, "You know, I always forget how good fresh fruit can be."

I wondered what she was going to eat when she got home.

After dinner we opened our presents.

Will looked really surprised when Uncle Max handed him a package to open. He ripped the paper off all at once. Didn't split the tape and keep it all nice like me and my mom. Well, like my mom. I just do it because she does it.

"Wow," he said. "That is so cool." He extended it to its full length. Only about four and a half feet. Whipped it back and forth and watched it whistle through the air. Sampson got scared and hid behind the couch. "It's so light."

"It's an ultralight," I said. "That's what you use for trout."

"That's so nice," he said. "That's so nice that you guys got me something. Something really nice." His face looked serious and deep. It worried me. It reminded me of the time he instant-messaged me and thanked me for being his friend. And I knew right away something was wrong. Because it isn't like Will to get mushy.

But the moment blew over because I opened my present from my mom. It was a big one, all right. It was amazing. It was this 49ers jacket with leather sleeves. This really warm, thick, padded black wool jacket with brown leather sleeves. And these SF patches and NFL patches and stuff. And on the back this special white oval patch sewn on, and on it was Terrell Owens's autograph. It was just the coolest thing I had ever seen in my life. I couldn't even talk. All I could do was stare at it with my mouth open and touch all the different parts of it, like I couldn't believe they were all true.

Uncle Max said, "I think he likes it, Lila."

The first words out of my mouth were not the very brightest. I think I was still in shock. Good shock, but shock. "Oh my God, it must've cost a fortune."

"You don't worry about that," my mother said. "You just enjoy it."

"Oh my God, it's amazing. It's the most amazing thing ever."

I got up and put it on, suddenly scared it wouldn't fit. Even though it was really big. What if I was bigger? It fit. It even snapped up. It was kind of tight around my stomach, but it had elastic at the waist anyway, so it didn't really matter. Much.

"This is the most amazing present I've ever gotten.

This is amazing." I knew I was saying the word amazing a lot, but I couldn't seem to stop. All of a sudden I was really glad I'd given the best Uncle Max present to Will. I would've felt so bad if I got that jacket and he got nothing, or even nothing very good.

"I can't take this up to the cabin, though. It'll get dirty."

"Nonsense," my mom said. "It's to wear, not to hang on the wall."

"But what if something happens to it? What if it gets messed up?"

"Then we get it cleaned."

"No, we can't get it cleaned, it might ruin the autograph."

"The autograph is done in permanent marker. It can be dry-cleaned."

"You're sure?"

"I checked."

I figured I would take it up there with me. But I wasn't sure I would wear it. I just wasn't sure I could bring myself to take a chance with it. What if I caught it on some barbed wire climbing over the fence? What if I hooked it with a fishhook or something?

But when I had to go back to school, then I'd wear it every day. All the time. Even in class. I felt like I'd be cool if I just wore that jacket all the time. Like I wouldn't even be the fat boy anymore. Or, anyway, like it wouldn't even matter that I was.

*   *   *

When Will and I were lying in the twin beds in Uncle Max's guest room that night, trying to get to sleep, Will said, "Did your uncle really get the rod and reel for me? Or did he just give it to me at the last minute so I'd have something to open?"

I hate to lie. But I made an exception. "He really got it for you," I said. "We talked about what to get you. He got you the rod so you'd have something to learn to trout-fish with. And so you can do it on your own if you like it."

I could hear Sampson snoring in the corner.

"Well, that was pretty nice. I thought maybe he got it for you, because . . . well, the fly-tying kit is okay, I guess. If you're into fly tying. But the rod really seems like a much better present."

"Yeah, but he knows I want to get into fly tying. Besides, he knew my mother was getting me something really big."

"Yeah, the jacket is cool. Even I think so, and I hate football. Your family is a lot better than the Manson family. Not that the Manson family sets the bar very high or anything. What if I don't like trout fishing, though?"

"You will," I said. "I know you will." I had to believe it. I felt like trout fishing could really save Will. Give him back something he loved to do, like saltwater fishing used to be. Before you-know-what happened. Besides, if he really loved it as much as I did, maybe he wouldn't want to take time off to go hunting. Maybe we could just fish the whole time. And maybe, just maybe . . . we could even talk for real.

We drove up to the cabin the next morning, which is up in the mountains, at like six thousand feet. The four of us. I say four because I'm counting Sampson. Good thing Uncle Max has an extra cab. Peaches didn't get to come. My mom would have been too lonely without Peaches for the holidays.

We had chains for the tires, just in case, but we were lucky. There was no snow.

I was wearing my new jacket, and I felt like a whole new me. But I was still worried a little about it, too, so I asked Uncle Max, "Did the jacket cost a fortune? I mean, can she afford this?"

"Let that be her worry, Ernie. Yes, she went all out, but that was her choice. She knows you've been having a rough time, and she wanted to do something special for you. She'll manage."

We stopped for gas at that little town where the gas station sells bait.

"How many cartons of worms should I get, Uncle Max?"

"Oh, if they have the twenty-five count, I'd say two. We can always get more down at the store by Marble Pools."

Will and I went in while Uncle Max filled the tank.

"Worms?" Will asked. "You fish for trout with worms?"

"You don't have to," I said. "You can use artificial bait. Power Bait. Or spinners. Or salmon eggs. But I always have the best luck with live night crawlers. Why? You have a problem with worms?"

"Well, they're just kind of gross is all."

"Oh, come on. This from a guy who hooks squid heads right between the eyes?"

"Yeah, but the squid is dead. It doesn't wiggle."

I rolled my eyes at him. "Fine. *I'll* bait the hooks."

"No, no. I'm not a total wimp. I'll deal with it."

While we were there, we also had to get a freshwater stamp for Will's fishing license, because his license was for salt water only.

While the lady was ringing us up, he lifted one of the lids off a worm carton and looked in. They always lie around on the top if they're good and fresh. I thought I saw him shudder just a little bit.

Turned out Will wasn't big on getting up early, so in the morning Uncle Max and I drove in his truck down to Brightwater Creek. Just as the sky was beginning to get light. So we could cast our lines into the water just when it was light enough for the trout to see our worms. That's the best time to fish. And it was nice, in a way, just me and Uncle Max, like in the old days. Like for as long as I can remember.

I caught one in the big, flat pool by the campground, and he caught two, all about twelve inches or so. Uncle Max has an old-fashioned creel, kind of a little wicker basket for fish, with a carrying strap. We put them in that and let it sit in the water.

It was cold at that hour. Man. Probably high twenties. I was wearing gloves with the fingers cut away, but when I had to handle a fish, it just left my fingers numb. I could hardly feel well enough to bait my hook again.

When it got light enough, Uncle Max asked if I felt like hiking up to the waterfall. That's, like, my favorite place in the whole, entire world. There's a trail up to it, so you don't have to rock-hop. We hiked up there, and the hike made me feel much warmer.

The waterfall is about fifty feet high, and it's really hard to get up above it. It can be done, if you don't mind sweating. Or getting scratched, or getting poison oak. But the best fishing pool I know is right at the base of it. Right at the back of the basin, where the waterfall carves out an extra-deep pool. I have no idea how deep it is, but it's just about deeper than any other part of the creek that I know of. Plus it's really bouldery up there, so I know there are lots of spaces for the fish to hide.

We baited our hooks again at the base of the falls. I looked up, and it was just as beautiful as I remembered. Green moss hanging down on the rocks, with three thin strands of water pouring down. I think I love the sound more than anything else. At the end of a good fishing day I like to lie in bed and remember the sound of the falling water.

I picked out a big, fat crawler so I could cast over to the deep part of the pool without having to artificially weight my line. I cast, and watched the worm land right where I wanted him to, right on that big dark patch that spells deep water. At first he just hung there under the surface, wiggling around. Then he sank, slowly, swishing his long body back and forth. I love to watch that. And so do the trout. I let out a little more line so he could go all the way to the bottom. Left my bail open the way I like to do. Next thing I know, more line was pulling off the reel. Three or four more wraps, like the line was swimming away. I love that moment. I snapped the bail shut, set the hook, and reeled in, waiting to see what I'd hooked. Hoping to see a great, giant natural brown. But what I saw was a rainbow. You can tell right away. There's a special flash to a rainbow. I pulled him all the way in and up out of the water, and he thrashed at the end of the hook, throwing droplets of freezing water into my face. I looked up and saw a little rainbow of colors in the mist thrown up by the waterfall. The other kind of rainbow.

"I bet you were hoping to see that big native brown," Uncle Max said.

I called him Moby, but only in my own head. I wouldn't tell Uncle Max that. It would sound silly. "Think he's still in here?"

"My neighbor two cabins over said he caught a twenty-inch brown in this pool."

My heart fell down. "Oh. He's gone, then."

"He threw it back."

"Really? You're not making it up?"

"I never lie to you, Ernie. I tell you the truth, not what I think you want to hear. He had so much respect for the fact that it lived to grow so big, without being caught, that he just couldn't bring himself to keep it. I told him how you caught that fish—or one just like it—last summer, but then it threw the hook just as you were bringing its head up out of the water."

"I would've kept him, though."

"Well, that's a decision we all have to make for ourselves."

I put my rainbow trout in the creel and cast in again. I got nibbles right away, but when I went to set my hook, there was nothing there. I reeled in to check my bait, and sure enough, it'd been stolen. I put on another worm and tried again.

This time we both just sat for a while, and nothing even nibbled. But it was so nice, just sitting there under the waterfall right after sunrise. I was happy whether I ever caught another fish or not.

Uncle Max said, "How's Will been doing since he got out of the hospital?"

"Hard to say. Because we don't really talk. I mean, we

talk. But not about that." We were almost whispering, because that's what you do around trout. "The only time he ever mentioned it—" Then I decided I shouldn't have started that sentence, and I didn't want to finish it.

Uncle Max doesn't push on stuff like that. He just said, "Up to you, Ernie."

"Well, he didn't sound real happy about the way it worked out. He didn't seem like he appreciated being saved. He acted like he really wanted to die. But I don't believe that, though. Because if he really wanted to die, he wouldn't have tipped me to what he was going to do."

"Sounded like a cry for help. I agree."

"Then why isn't he glad I helped him?"

"I don't know. Maybe he is and he can't admit it. Maybe he will be later. That's not the important part anyway. The important part is, do you think you did the right thing?"

"Oh, absolutely. Yeah."

"Then that has to be enough."

After that we just fished quietly for another twenty minutes or so, but we didn't get so much as a nibble. But we had four nice ones in the creel, so Uncle Max said, "I think they've just plain stopped biting. Let's go back and have breakfast with what we've got. When Will's eaten trout this fresh for breakfast, then maybe he'll be happy to be alive."

"That just might do it," I said.

Thing is, we were only about half kidding.

* * *

About noon Will and I went fishing up by the waterfall at Brightwater Creek. I just really wanted to show him that. Him being from L.A. and all, I wasn't sure he knew places that beautiful could even exist.

Uncle Max drove us down in his truck and gave us quarters for the pay phone at the campground, so we could call when we needed a ride back. And he packed us a good lunch. Big turkey sandwiches on whole wheat bread, with cranberry sauce.

We started out in the big pool down by the campground, but it did not go well. To put it mildly. We'd made the mistake of taking Sampson with us. Seemed like a good idea at the time. We walked right up to that pool, and Will sucked in his breath, and I could tell he was amazed to just see the trout gliding around under the water.

Unfortunately, Sampson saw them, too, and went diving right in. Galloped around in the pool, which is mostly less than two feet deep, biting into the water like he could catch one. Of course, by the time his front paws hit the water, the trout had all run to cover. So he didn't catch one. And now neither would we.

Then he leaped out again, like he really surprised himself by how cold it was.

Sampson was a big, silly-looking yellow mutt. He looked like he had a lot of golden retriever or golden Lab, but then something wirehaired, too. So he had a kind of a stiff beard. Which was dripping wet. He shook himself and sprayed freezing creek water over both of us. Good thing I wasn't wearing my new jacket.

I leaned over a fallen log and looked into the pond. Not a trout in sight. Like they all moved and left no forwarding address.

"Well, that won't help," I said.

"Won't they come out again?"

"Well, eventually."

"How long a memory can a trout have?"

"They're just very spooky creatures. You have no idea how easy it is to scare them off. I think we need to climb up to a higher pool. And this time we need to tie that dog up. Come on. I want to show you the waterfall anyway."

We hiked up there, puffing a little. Well, I was puffing a lot. I had all the tackle in my backpack. Will just had his new rod, collapsed and sticking out of the waistband of his jeans. The sandwich was burning a hole in my pocket, so I ate half of it on the way up. When we got up there, his mouth fell wide open. At first I didn't even look at the waterfall. I just looked at Will looking at the waterfall.

He said, "That's the most beautiful thing I've ever seen in my life."

I wanted to say, See? Now aren't you glad you're still around to see it? But I didn't, of course. I wanted to, but I didn't. I kept seeing moments to talk for real, but then they went by. I don't know why I couldn't just say what I wanted to say to him.

Will just kept going. "I thought places like this were only in pictures. Oh, that's a stupid thing to say. I didn't mean that exactly. I just mean I thought *I'd* only ever see a thing like that in a picture. I never thought I'd *be* in a place like this."

While he was talking, I put a worm on his hook.

He looked down. "Oh. Thank you." He sounded kind of surprised, like he just woke up or something. He was holding Sampson's collar. Then he came around, like shaking himself awake, and tied Sampson to a tree with my chain stringer.

"Try to cast over to the waterfall. It's deepest right underneath. That's where all the good fish are. But be gentle when you cast. If you put too much of a snap on it, you'll knock the worm right off there."

"Okay." He swung the rod back and forth a few times to get the feel of it. Then he cast in a nice, high arc, and the worm actually landed on one of the rocks under the falls. So he reeled it in a couple of turns, and it dropped right into deep water.

I bent down to bait my own hook, but before I even could, Will said, "I got a bite! I got a bite already!"

I watched as it came through the water, and my heart just sank. He was reeling in an enormous natural brown. A good twenty inches. Will had caught Moby.

"He's big. He's bending my rod almost in half."

"Loosen the drag a little. It's only a four-pound line. A

fish that big could break it. Don't worry about the rod. It's flexible. It won't break."

I watched him fight that fish in, thinking, There's lots that could still go wrong. Moby could break the line, or wiggle off the hook. It happens. It happened to me. The question was, did I want it to happen to Will?

No. That's what I decided. No. I wanted Will to catch Moby. I got to come up here all the time. I also got the best Christmas present, and the good family. I even got the lingcod. Will never even caught a legal ling, and when he finally did, he had to give it to me and pretend he didn't. Even though something in my stomach still didn't like it, I decided I was willing to let Will have Moby.

He pulled him up and out of the water. Holy cow, what a beauty. Speckled dark brown with a silvery belly. Biggest trout I ever saw with my own eyes. A trout is just the most beautiful fish in the world to me. Moby was the most beautiful trout.

"Careful," I said. "He can still come off the hook. Turn him away from the water so he won't fall back into the pool if he comes free. Here, I'll get the towel."

When I turned back with the towel, Moby had shaken the hook and fallen onto the ground. I threw Will the towel, and he dove down to grab him. But the fish gave one huge, thrashing flip of his body and landed in the water. Will was looking at his hands, like he couldn't believe the fish wasn't in them. Then we both just stood there and watched him swim away. It was heartbreaking.

"I can't believe I lost him. I had him. I just had him."

"I lost that same fish last summer. Either that or his identical twin. I still haven't gotten over it."

"Gee, thanks. Here I was telling myself I'd feel better in a little while."

I baited his hook again, and my own, and we both cast back into the deep water under the falls. We both got hits right away. We were both reeling in at the same time. Two rainbows, ten or eleven inches long. They came all the way in, too.

I took them both off the hooks carefully and put them in Uncle Max's creel.

"Well, that's something, anyway," Will said. "At least I caught something. What're the chances that same fish would bite again?"

"Not too good, I wouldn't think. You hear about fish that're so stupid they'll get caught twice in one day. But I think they're hardly ever trout."

I caught another one about ten minutes later. A brown, but not a huge brown. Big enough, I guess.

Then I looked down and saw a good-sized brown hanging out in the shallow part of the pool, right near us. I pointed him out to Will. Quietly.

"Where?" he whispered.

"Right there."

"I don't see it. Oh, yes I do!"

They're pretty well camouflaged. Until they move, you might not even see them.

Will reeled in and then cast his worm right in front of that fish, and he followed the bait. I could feel Will holding his breath while the fish poked at that worm.

"I can't believe I'm watching this. I've never fished for fish I could see."

"Be patient," I whispered.

He was. Until the worm was gone. Then he set the hook and reeled him in. Will was so excited he just couldn't contain himself. He had never in his whole life looked down through crystal clear water and watched himself catch a fish.

Then we caught at the same time again, but mine was only about eight inches, so I kept him in the water while I pulled the hook out of his mouth, and I let him swim away.

Will asked if there was a size limit.

I said, "No, but the bag limit is five. So I can only catch one more."

"Hey, math genius, one more would make three."

"But I caught two this morning. It's five per angler per day."

"Nobody's going to know that! If we get stopped, they won't see the two you caught this morning. We ate them, remember? No one will ever know."

I shrugged my shoulders. "I'll know."

He just shook his head at me. "Then I'm going to catch

seven. That way we'll be heading back with ten for the two of us. Or are you going to turn me in if I do that?"

I shrugged again. "No. It's just one of those decisions we all have to make for ourselves, I guess."

It didn't matter anyway, because Will didn't catch seven. I caught my three and he caught four, and then they just stopped biting. When you're not used to trout fishing, you don't get that. You're reeling them in like crazy, and you think you can do that all day. But they either bite or they don't, and sometimes they just stop and other times they just start. And nobody really knows when or why. Believe me, if anybody knew the solution to that mystery, they'd bottle it and sell it to fishermen all over the world.

We packed up to go, and Will opened the creel and looked in at our seven fish. Five rainbows and two browns. We didn't know whose were whose anymore, and probably didn't even care.

"Wish I hadn't lost that big one," he said. "That would've been so cool, to show your uncle Max that. But these are good, I guess. They're so beautiful. Trout are such a beautiful fish." He ran a finger down one of the fish's slippery sides.

In my head I thought, Say it. Tell him we need to talk for real. Tell him you're worried about him. That things are taking a bad turn. Tell him you brought him out here because something needs to change before we go back to school, otherwise just about anything could happen.

"Yeah, trout are beautiful," I said. And kicked myself all the way down.

We fired up the barbecue and cooked the fish out on the back deck, on the grill, pressed into one of those fish baskets that keep the trout from falling apart when you turn them. It was nearly dark already. Will and I were sitting out on the deck, watching the moon rise over the mountains. This nearly full moon. And keeping an eye on the fish. The cabin is on a meadow, one of the High Sierra meadows, and this light mist of fog was lying down in the center of the meadow, but you could still see the stars come out above it. You could still see the early night sky.

I was wearing my new jacket.

Will said, "Trout is the best-tasting fish I ever ate, too. I know you probably thought I just said that for your uncle's sake. But I really meant it. I never thought I'd eat fish for breakfast. But that was the best breakfast ever."

We sat and looked at the first stars a minute longer. Now and then the breeze shifted, and we had to wave smoke out of our eyes.

Then Will said, "I'm sorry about that thing I said to you."

"Which thing?" But he looked a little hurt, so I said, "I didn't mean to make it sound like you say lots of bad things. I just don't know what you said."

"I'm sorry I said you should've let me die. That wasn't

true. Well, maybe I thought it was at the time. But now I'm glad you didn't."

I didn't answer, because I figured that was all that needed to be said about that. We just sat there and watched the stars come out, and waited for our dinner to be ready.

Just before I got up to turn the fish, Will said, "I just realized something. This is what people are talking about when they say they're happy. How are we supposed to go back, though? I wish we didn't have to go back."

"I refuse to worry about that on the second day of our vacation." After all, we still had time for things to change.

He nodded, like he agreed. But he still looked worried.

Much as Will loved to fish for trout, the hunting issue would not go away.

It actually took us two days. One to teach me to shoot and for Uncle Max to satisfy himself that we understood gun safety, and another to actually go out in the woods and find a deer.

The morning Uncle Max took us up into the forest was Christmas morning. And it was snowing. And early, and cold. But there was something about being outdoors on a morning like that, on a white Christmas in California, just being out in the middle of that perfect, untouched blanket of snow. It also made it almost impossible to get lost. We could always follow our own footsteps back to the truck.

This'll sound weird, but Will and I were tied together. Uncle Max tied a short piece of rope through my belt loop and then Will's. He took our safety pretty seriously. And if we could never get more than about a foot apart, it would be nearly impossible to shoot each other.

It took us over an hour and a half to find a deer. When Will spotted a young buck, we were comfortably tucked behind a boulder, where he wasn't likely to spot us back. Uncle Max was about twenty paces back, just making sure we were okay.

I looked at the buck, and I was just blown away by how beautiful he was. And how much I didn't want to shoot him. Which is funny, because I was blown away by how beautiful trout were, too. But I caught them anyway. But trout were different. They breathed water. They were cold-blooded. They didn't have warm fur and warm hearts and draw breath through perfect black nostrils.

We didn't dare say a word, but I made a gesture to say, You. You take him. After all, Will is the one who loves to hunt. But he shook his head and handed it back to me, all without a word. After all, he was introducing me to hunting, and the least he could do was let me give it a try.

I raised the rifle and peered at the buck through the scope. He was no less beautiful. I could feel my hands shake a little bit. Then I raised the muzzle of the rifle a hair higher and purposely fired a shot over his back. The shot slammed through the cold air and echoed around again. I dropped the rifle and watched the buck leap away. Well, leap anyway. He leaped into the air, and then a second shot hit my eardrums. The buck just seemed to freeze that way for a split second, a foot or two above the snow. Then he fell onto his knees and crumpled onto his chin, his eyes open.

We ran through the snow to him, but it wasn't easy, because we were still tied together. We found him bleeding into the snow from a perfect round red hole in his shoulder. Will was a good shot.

"I missed," I said.

If Will knew I missed on purpose, he never said so. He might've known, though.

Will ran a hand down the buck's side, like he was worshipping something. The blood steamed when it hit the snow.

I'm never going to be a hunter, I know that now. I don't know why it should be so different. Like Will said, I eat meat. But if I had to look into its big, wet-looking dark eye and then shoot it first, I'd live the rest of my life on peanut butter, pasta, and fish. I just admired the deer too much.

I felt Uncle Max's hand on my shoulder. "Good shooting on someone's part."

"It was Will," I said. "I missed him."

"Excellent job, Will."

Will turned to Uncle Max and threw his arms around him, half dragging me along. I didn't know if it was because he took us hunting, or because he told Will he did a good job on something. I'm not sure anybody ever tells Will that. I'm not sure anybody ever did.

Uncle Max was surprised. He's not a real touchy-feely kind of guy. Then again, neither is Will. At first Uncle Max just stood there with his arms at his sides. Giving me this look, like, What did I say?

Will said, "Thank you for this vacation."

Uncle Max clapped him on the back and said, "You are very welcome."

Then he handed Will his hunting knife and untied the rope that held us together, and they wrestled the buck over onto his back. Will made a big cut down the middle of his belly. I heard a rush of warm air, and smelled blood, and watched a cloud of steam rise.

At first I wanted to look away, but I didn't. It was life. After all. So I watched him pull out the stomach and guts, and cut out the area under his tail, and leave all that in the snow for whatever animals would come along. I watched him reach up for the lungs and heart, pushing back his sleeves and getting bloody to the elbows.

"I don't like liver," he said to Uncle Max, holding it in his hands.

"I'll eat the liver."

"I don't have anything to put it in, though."

"Put it back in the body cavity when you're done."

Then I watched Will go in under the hip bone, going

after the bladder. Not that I knew what he was going for. But Uncle Max asked if he knew to be careful how he cut and how hard he pulled, and Will smiled and said, "Yeah, it's not like I've never gotten a face full," and Uncle Max smiled.

I felt like they were speaking a language I couldn't understand, and it made me feel left out and sad.

Then they cut a long branch and tied the buck's legs together, and slid the branch through and hoisted it up on their shoulders, and we all hiked back to the truck. Silent, not saying a word. Not needing to.

I was clumping along behind, thinking, That's really *my* uncle Max. Not yours. But it was a little like the giant brown trout. Will had so little. Not that it meant I should give him my uncle Max exactly. But it wouldn't kill me to loan him out for a while.

Good thing I came to that conclusion, because it took them two and a half hours to finish dressing that thing out and cutting it up. I heard Will skinned it, too, and hung the skin in the shed, so it wouldn't draw animals in the night. I heard he was going to tan that skin and keep it. But I didn't see any of it with my own eyes. I chose not to watch. I knew we'd be having venison for dinner, and I'd seen enough of the insides of that buck. I passed on seeing the skinned flesh.

Besides, I did enough to help. I loaned him my uncle

Max. I practiced tying flies for two and a half hours and stayed out of their way.

That night Will and I pulled lounge chairs out on the back deck and lay on them in sleeping bags, looking up at the stars. It was a perfect, clear night. I'd told Will I bet he didn't even know how many stars there really were, and he had no idea what I meant, so we lay out there and shivered in our sleeping bags and took it all in.

Will was being quiet, but in a good sort of way. I knew he felt good. Settled. In a way I could never understand, he found himself in the hunting. I didn't feel it, but I didn't mind if he did. He didn't get that many chances to find himself, or to feel good.

"You're right," he said. "It's maybe four times as many stars as I thought."

"It's the city lights. They fade out the sky. Plus it's a really clear night."

"It's not completely clear. There's that little soft band of cloud right along there."

"That's the edge of the Milky Way."

"No way."

"Way."

"That band there?"

"Yup. The edge of our galaxy."

He drifted back into that satisfied silence.

I let that ride for a couple of minutes. Then I said, "Are

we ever gonna talk about Sam?" Surprised the hell out of myself. I had no idea I was about to say that.

He didn't answer for a long time, and I didn't look at him. I was thinking maybe it was a mistake to bring it up. After a time I heard a sniff, and I knew he was crying. At first I felt really bad, but then I thought, All that stuff is in there anyway. It might as well come out.

"I'm sorry if it's a sore subject," I said. "I just keep thinking that if you could talk about what happened, then you wouldn't have had to do something terrible to yourself to get help. I mean, do you still feel like it was your fault?"

Another long silence. Oh well, I thought. At least I tried. Uncle Max would say, Then that has to be enough.

"I do and I don't," he said, and it surprised me. "I know I didn't mean for it to happen. I never meant any harm to the kid. But I should've sat up when you said to sit up. I mean, I had that ling on the stringer. And I had the stringer wrapped around my hand. He wasn't going anywhere. All I had to do was sit up until the swell passed. And then go back to cutting him loose again. I think about that when I go to bed at night. And I wake up at night thinking about it. I have dreams, too. In my dreams at night I hear you saying, 'Will, sit up, there's a big swell coming.' Sometimes I dream it out a different way, where I sit up. And the swell just kind of splashes us, and then I bring the fish in, and we catch a bunch more. And then we motor back to shore, and Sam is fine, and everything's fine. And I finally caught that big ling, and my father's boat isn't gone, and he doesn't have to go to jail. And my mother doesn't have to come live with me and bring that creep with her. And I don't have to try to kill myself and you don't get pitched down the stairs while I'm gone. And it's just all okay. It could've been that way. I know now what I had to do to make it be that way. And it's so easy. Just sit up. And now I want to, like . . . I want to rewind to that moment and do it right. How do you do that, Ernie? How do you rewind life?"

"Um. You don't." Should I have backed up and corrected that part about getting pitched down the stairs? I don't know. I just know I didn't.

"Right. You don't. Why didn't I sit up? Am I just stupid? Or am I a little bit crazy like everybody says?"

"I don't think either. I just think when you really love to fish like we do, your brain sort of locks up at that big moment. You know you caught something good, and it's like an obsession. Your brain locks on it, and you just can't think about anything else."

We were quiet for a long time. I felt small looking up at the stars. The world looked so big, and Will and I were just like nothing. In the whole big scheme.

Then he said, "See, this is why you're my best friend, Ernie. Because you get it. You actually get what I mean. Other people just look at me like I'm nuts."

I was struggling with how to take a compliment, but then it didn't matter, because he just kept going.

"Sometimes I think it's not even that moment I blame myself for. It's more like everything before it. I was so hateful to him. It's like when he was born. As soon as he was born, I hated him. Because I already had nothing. I mean, whatever you're supposed to give a kid so he can grow up, I had nothing. And then this little snot-nose comes along and I'm supposed to divide nothing in half and share it with him? And that was when he was born. Later it got even worse. When I found out he was cuter, and they were going to like him better than me. I know he was a really bad, snotty little kid. But sometimes I think, What if I hadn't been so hateful to him? What if I'd acted like he was really my brother? Maybe he would've turned out all different."

I don't really think you can blame yourself for what your brother grows up to be, but I never had one, so I didn't feel qualified to say.

"It does help to talk about this," Will said.

But we didn't, after that night.

We spent another week like that, catching our limit every day. Will tanned his deerskin and made a bunch of venison jerky. Froze what he didn't dry. We made fires in the fireplace at night, and Uncle Max would come out of his room and tell us stories about his travels. He writes nonfiction books about other countries, so he can tell you things like what Afghanistan was like long before the Russian invasion, long before the Taliban came in and we chased them out again. He can tell you what Iran was like back when they called it Persia.

I could listen to him all night, but I thought it was just me. But Will could listen all night, too. I think something shifted in Will when he found out Uncle Max didn't hate him. Will thinks everybody hates him. Unfortunately, he's usually right.

Will loved trout fishing so much that he even learned how to tie flies.

But by the time we had to go home, whatever good had come out of him seemed to go back into hiding again.

On the drive home he was quiet. Too quiet. Something about his face seemed dark. He never once talked on the ride home. Uncle Max would say things to try to get him to chat, but all he would do was grunt.

When we dropped him at his house, there was no one there. He had to go in with a key, and we helped him carry in all his stuff, and all his packages of frozen venison, wrapped in white butcher paper, that we brought back in Uncle Max's cooler. And the packets of jerky. Only about two-thirds of the frozen stuff would go in their freezer, though, so he gave some venison to Uncle Max and some to me.

And then we just left him there. What choice did we have?

I guess maybe he was happy to be home alone. I mean, if he had to be home at all. But he was definitely feeling moody, and I know we were both worried about him.

As soon as we walked out of his house, Uncle Max said, "Anything happen I don't know about? What's so terrible that all that good mood just disappeared?"

I said, "It's nothing you don't know about. He just didn't want to go home."

"Oh."

"I thought it would really help him to take him up there and let him have a vacation and be happy. You know? And he really was. But now that he knows what it's like to be happy, I think it might be even harder for him to go back to his life."

"He must've been happy sometime."

"I'm not so sure," I said.

Actually, I'm pretty sure. I think he never was.

January 5th

Today was our first day back at school. Call it denial, but I really wasn't braced. I mean, I hated to be back. But I didn't expect things to fall apart so fast.

Because, you know, before we left for vacation, things were pretty quiet. Will was still all brittle, and nobody wanted to be the one to break him for real, and everybody pretty much stayed out of our way.

And also, I know this sounds stupid, but I really thought it would be better in that jacket. I thought I'd be something a little different. A little more. I know it's weird to think like that, and looking back on it, it seems like a stupid way to feel, but that's how I went into the day.

I think the reason it all went to hell so fast was Will.

There was something different about him. And it's hard to describe what it was. He was mad, though. He was mad to be home, and to have to go to school. He was upset about being in his life. And for some reason it wasn't a helpless, passive sort of a problem. He was really projecting a lot of trouble.

We were in second period. Mr. Gregorio's history class. And one of the jocks kept staring at Will. Except I think Will might've started it. And also Will kept staring right back, which is like a total rookie mistake. It was that red-haired guy. Usually he's not one of the really bad ones. Usually he's not as bad as the other four. He just stands there with them and laughs. But Will challenged him, and he challenged right back, from two seats in front. While we were supposed to be taking a test.

It's one of those things like glancing nervously over your shoulder. Or maybe it's just the opposite. One says you can be put in your place really easy, the other says you deserve to be. But either way it's like bleeding into the water. Like, Here, sharky, sharky, sharky. You almost never have to ask them twice.

I looked up just in time to see Red Jock turn toward Will—turn his head so Mr. Gregorio wouldn't see him—and do the fish imitation.

I got icy cold all over, and my heart pounded. Sure, they've been doing it to us forever. But this was different. This was now. This was after Will's little brother died with those fishes.

Did he not know? Did he not care? Did he somehow not know that Will would see it as a clear message? A mortal insult? He might just as well have captioned the move, "What's this? The last thing your little brother ever saw."

Because I know that's what Will heard.

Will took off through the air and landed swinging. Really clumsy swings, meant to batter the jock in the head, but most of them swung wild.

A lot of kids jumped up from their desks to get out of the way, and I heard Mr. Gregorio yell, "Hey!" And then I saw Will fly through the air again, only not by choice this time. Red Jock just sort of flipped him away, and he landed hard on a desk on his side, and ended up on the floor, and came up like he'd hurt himself. Like he couldn't really straighten up all the way.

He still tried to go back in for more, though, but Mr. Gregorio grabbed him around the waist and held him and said, "What the hell is wrong with you, Will?"

He stopped fighting then.

See, that was a bad choice of words. If he'd said, What's gotten into you? or, Why are you acting this way? But the idea that there was something wrong with Will was getting pretty widespread, and hearing it from the mouth of a teacher just stole all the rest of Will's air. Probably nobody else in the room was aware of all that but me. It was painfully clear to me, though.

Mr. Gregorio sent him down to the principal's office

and said he'd be down right after the bell, so don't think about going anywhere else.

Will walked out looking like he'd lost the war.

That's when it hit me. Nobody had my back. I was down behind enemy lines alone.

After the bell, I was trying to get out without incident, but Mr. Gregorio stopped me. "Wait," he said.

And I did, because I had no choice, but I was dying to stay with the crowd. If he kept me too long, I might end up in a nearly empty hall. It could get ugly out there alone.

"Yes, sir?"

"Is there some explanation behind what just happened? Because it looked like Will flipped out and tried to beat somebody up for no reason at all. Was there something more to it? Something I didn't see?"

I looked up and saw three of the jocks standing out in the hall. Rusty and one of the others whose name I don't know, and the red guy. Waiting to see what I would say.

Mr. Gregorio had his back turned to them, but he saw me looking, and he looked over his shoulder. And they quick stopped staring and just started talking to each other, like there was nothing going on at all. Mr. Gregorio went over and closed the door.

I had a bad choice to make. Was I actually going to rat one of them out? That had to spell certain death. But the only other choice was to betray Will and say he did what he did for no reason, which was like the last thing he needed at a time like this, when people seriously thought he might be losing it anyway. Besides, even if I didn't rat the jock out, they would think I did, and I'd probably be dead the minute I walked out into the hall. No matter what I said.

I had to steady myself by thinking what Uncle Max would tell me to do. The right thing. Obviously. He'd tell me to do what I think is right.

I said, "That guy was teasing Will. He did this thing they've been doing to us forever. Making fun of us for liking fishing. But he might've meant it to pick on Will about how his brother died. Or, at least . . . I mean, even if he didn't mean it that way, I know Will thought he did."

Mr. Gregorio nodded a little and chewed on the inside of his lip. "Hmm," he said. "I'd better tell that to the principal, because it might make a difference in the length of his suspension."

My gut tingled at the sound of that word. Suspension. I wasn't alone behind enemy lines for a period or two. I was here for weeks.

"I'll have a talk with Harris."

Right. That was the red guy's name. Harris Tripp.

He stepped out of the classroom and into the hall. Leaving the door wide open. I wondered if I should slip by them all now and get away. But Mr. Gregorio hadn't said I could go yet. I could hear him talking to the three jocks. Not exactly hear his words. Not from where I sat, on a desk in the front row, willing it to bear my weight. Pretending I didn't have to walk out into the hall. Ever. But I could hear there were words. Just not exactly what they were.

After a while he came back in. Back to where I was sitting.

"He swears he didn't know," he told me.

"Everybody knows about Will's brother."

"He says he knew he died. He says he knew it was drowning. But he figured it was a pool accident or something more like that."

"Do you believe him?" Meaning, should I?

"Hard to imagine anybody would purposely pick on Will over a thing like that. He actually sounded pretty sorry when I told him how it came out."

"Why would anyone pick on him at all? Over anything? After everything that's happened?"

"Good question," he said. "People don't think. They don't use their heads." I didn't answer, so he waited a second and then said, "Okay, thanks." Like, You can go now.

But I really didn't want to go out there alone. "Ah . . . are you going down to the office now?"

"In a minute," he said. "I'll go down in a minute."

I sighed. And walked out to meet my fate.

They were there, of course. The three of them. There were a few other people around, but that never helped me much in the past.

I tried to walk down the hall to my next class, but they got in front of me and blocked me off. My face felt hot.

"Look," I said. "Just leave me alone, okay? Just get out of my way and let me go to my class."

"Yeah, sure, Fat Boy," Rusty said. "We'll do that." He put one hand in the middle of my chest, stopping me from moving forward. "But first I have a question to ask. Why are you wearing my jacket?"

I got so scared that the sounds in the hall got far off, like when you're falling asleep. Like the world was moving farther away. All of a sudden dying seemed like getting off easy. Nothing could be worse than this.

"I'm not. It's mine."

"Oh no it's not. That's *my* jacket. Now take it off and give it to me."

"No!" I said it not so much like standing up for myself. More like, No, anything but that! It was a big, weak, helpless no, and it drew them like the predators they were.

I felt them grab at my arms and try to pull off the sleeves. I pulled my arms in close to my sides and tried to keep them in, but those guys were strong. So I fell down on the floor in a fetal position and tried to lie on my arms and keep the jacket all around me, but I felt their hands underneath me, pulling my arms out. I felt a sleeve pulled off one arm, and I tried to roll onto as much of the jacket as I could, but I got the sinking feeling that I was losing fast. It was just a matter of time.

So I did something I've never done before. And never, ever thought I would. I screamed for help. And I do mean screamed. I screamed so loud it hurt my throat to force out those three words. Three words I don't think I've ever said before in my life.

"Somebody help me!"

Mr. Gregorio came running out of his room.

The two jocks who weren't holding my jacket took off running. I looked up to see Rusty standing over me, still holding most of the jacket. I still had one sleeve on.

He dipped his head closer to me. "I don't believe you did that. You are so dead."

I remembered when Will started carrying the pepper spray. And how at the time I was thinking that they don't actually, literally kill you. That was still true, right? I mean, I knew it was. But I had to keep reminding myself. Because that "so dead" was really creepy. Whatever it literally meant, it was a very chilling thing.

"What's happening here?" Mr. Gregorio yelled.

It was too late to act like I didn't just scream for help after all. So I said, "They were trying to steal my new jacket. My mother gave me this jacket for Christmas."

Rusty let go of the jacket, and I quick put it back on.

Mr. Gregorio said, "Is there something in the water today, or what? I've never seen you guys so out of control."

But that's only because most of the time he doesn't see it. Because most of the time I would never dare scream for help.

Then he said, "Well, it's convenient that I was just headed to the office anyway."

He grabbed Rusty by the arm and kind of towed him off down the hall. I watched Rusty stumble a step or two behind. He turned around and caught my eye and then ran one finger across his throat, like he was cutting it with a knife. Very clear message: You are dead. Your life is over. Figuratively speaking. Like I said before. Like I kept telling myself. They don't kill you. They just make you wish you were dead.

I didn't doubt him, either. From that moment forward I'm figuratively dead boy walking.

I took off my jacket and locked it in my locker, where nothing bad could happen to it. But I still worried about it. I worried I'd come back and the lock would be cut or broken. And it would be gone. Or, worse yet, ruined. Covered in paint or cut to ribbons. They might do that. Because this was escalating with every unfortunate misstep. On both sides. And because I had made the fatal mistake of letting them know how much it meant to me.

Between classes I'd stick my head around the corner and look down the hall at my locker, but everything still looked okay.

When I got to gym class, I slipped into Mr. Bayliss's office and out of my clothes. Stripped down to just my boxer shorts. I looked at the scale. I had a feeling I'd lost a little since my vacation at Uncle Max's cabin. It seemed like the waistband of my jeans didn't cut me in half quite as bad as what I was used to. And it made sense that I would lose up there. I got lots more exercise than usual, and ate mostly venison and trout.

I got on the scale: 236.

It hit me that I could probably always lose weight at Uncle Max's cabin. But could I keep it off at home? That was the big question.

I ran into Mr. Bayliss on the way into the gym.

"How's our little deal going?" he asked.

"Okay," I said. "I lost six pounds."

He gave me a good slap on the back and said, "Way to go, Ernie boy."

In a way it felt good. In another way it was kind of pathetic. Six down, over ninety-five to go. No one would even notice six. And I didn't even know if I could keep from putting it right back on again now that I was home.

But I guess you have to start somewhere.

At the end of the day I took the jacket back, rolled it up inside out, and held it close to my body while I got home as fast as I could. And it went fine. Because this was an easy day. Rusty was suspended, and the other guys probably left school entirely to avoid the flap. It was like a tiny, quiet little no-man's-land.

I knew it could never last.

Will was sitting on my front steps when I got home.

"Why are you here?" I asked, not like I really minded, just curious.

He just shrugged, and I knew he couldn't bring himself to go home.

I let us both in with my key and got us glasses of milk and a couple of pieces of the chocolate cake my mom had made to welcome me home. I took them into my room. Will had his shirt off, and he was looking at his side in the mirror. I never saw him with his shirt off before. He was even bonier than I thought. His whole side was just this massive purple bruise.

"That looks bad," I said.

"I think I might've broken a rib. Or cracked one or something. It hurts to breathe all the way in."

"Are you gonna tell your mom? Get it x-rayed?"

He shook his head. "The less I tell my mom, the better."

He put his shirt back on, and we sat down and ate the cake and drank the milk. There was something quiet and solid coming up in Will. Usually solid is a good thing, though. This wasn't good. This was upsetting.

"How long are you suspended for?"

"Just three days."

"Oh. Good. Maybe I should get sick for three days. Because I'm gonna die if I go back to school without you."

I started to tell him about Harris Tripp. How he didn't

know Sam died fishing. But I didn't. He would never believe it anyway. And I wasn't sure enough to convince him.

Instead I just told him the story about the jacket.

He stopped chewing and just listened with his mouth open. "If they do something to that jacket," he said, weirdly calm, "I'll kill them. I'm serious."

"I hope that's just talk," I said.

"It's less just talk every day."

"It scares the crap out of me when you say things like that, Will. I really wish you wouldn't say things like that. You're letting them pull you down to their level. We're better than all that."

He jumped up, knocking his half-full milk glass over onto my rug. "That's what I'm saying, Ernie, that's my point. We're better than this. Why do we let them treat us like this?"

I was looking around for something to wipe up the milk with. A shirt that was on its way to the hamper anyway, or something like that. Meanwhile, Peaches was licking most of it off the rug. "Because we have no choice," I said. "They're the hunters, we're the hunted." The minute it came out of my mouth, I regretted the phrasing.

"You think I'm not a hunter?"

"I didn't mean—"

"We let them treat us like animals. We avert our eyes. Put our tail between our legs. Why?"

"Because otherwise they hurt us even worse."

"And then we do what? Cower harder. We never make

it worse for them. We never come back even harder at them."

"Now you're talking about a blood feud. And I don't want any part of that."

"I'm talking about justice," he said. He was still standing, his arms in the air like he was leading an orchestra. A little smear of chocolate on his lip.

"You're talking about letting them turn us into violent idiots. So then how are we any different from them?"

"Because we would never do that to someone innocent. Someone who never did a thing to us. It's like the difference between a cold-blooded killer and the person who gives him the lethal injection."

"Funny you should mention that," I said, "because I have trouble with that distinction, too."

He deflated back to more or less normal size and sat down. "See, that's your problem, Ernie. You're too softhearted."

"I don't think I am. Especially when you consider the opposite of softhearted is hard-hearted. If they stole my jacket, or ruined it, you think it would help if you committed some kind of violence against them? Wouldn't it be smarter to just make sure they don't get their hands on it?"

"I just don't think we should have to live like this," he said.

I wanted to say something, but no matter how long we sat there eating cake, I never thought of what to say. Because, really, he was right. Just that last sentence, I mean. We hadn't done anything to anyone, and we didn't deserve to live like this. But here we were. "Let's just put our energy into this three-day stomach flu I'm about to get," I said. Then, after a minute of watching him out of the corner of my eye, "Promise me you won't take this the wrong way. Because you know I'm your friend and all. But do you think maybe it's time to stop blowing off those therapy appointments?"

I thought he would get sore again, but he stayed calm. "I don't know if that would do any good."

"Well, of course you don't know. You've never gone. I'm just thinking you won't know unless you try it."

He nodded twice. Didn't answer at first. But after a minute or two he said, "I'll think about it. You know why they won't let you have that jacket, right?"

"Sure, because they know it's important to me. Once they know that, they know how to get to me."

"It's more than that. It's a nice thing. It's something good. Something they'd actually want for themselves. And they can't let you have something good. They can't let you step up. They won't let your life get better. It's all about holding us down."

I didn't answer. I actually thought he might be right, but I never said so.

It hit me, possibly for the first time ever, that even if I could lose a hundred pounds, it might not help. Maybe they wouldn't let me keep that victory, either.

January 6th

As soon as my mom had gone off to work, I called Will, and he came right over. Brought a bunch of venison jerky. Just to break up the flow of peanut butter and jelly sandwiches, he said. But it was more than that. He'd taken that deer with his own two hands, it was the first thing he'd done right in a long time, and it meant something to him. He needed the reminder of that moment of glory. I wondered what he would do when it was gone. I guess that's what the tanned skin was for.

We spent the morning playing video games and chewing on jerky. It was a little tangier than beef jerky, but otherwise not so different. Some sheets were a little stringy and some were okay. After a while my jaw got tired, but I didn't say so.

Between games, he said, just out of nowhere, "If you keep the jacket in your locker, they'll go in after it."

"I know. But I can't leave it home or my mom will think I don't like it. That would almost be worse than if it got stolen or ruined."

"Here's the plan. You keep your old jacket at my house. I'll walk over and pick you up in the morning. But instead of walking straight to school, we can go by my house. You can change and leave the good jacket in my closet until after school."

"That actually sounds good," I said. I was relieved. More than I could ever bring myself to say. I really had no good ideas until he said that.

"It's still totally unfair. Because if you don't get to wear it, it's like they win. They succeeded in not letting you have it. But we need a temporary plan, and that'll do. It'll get fixed for real. Soon enough. You'll see."

"How?"

"You'll see."

"I get nervous when you say things like that."

He just changed the subject, though. "My jaws are getting tired from eating nothing but jerky all morning. What else have you got around here?"

I knew anything my mom bought would be superfattening. And I had some big repenting to do after the number I did on that chocolate cake. If you didn't offer me those things, I might be okay. But if it's right there, I can't seem to say no.

"There's venison in the freezer." I was mostly kidding. I didn't think he was looking for a venison steak to break up a day of nothing but venison jerky.

"Perfect," he said. "I'll cook."

"You can cook?"

"I can cook venison. If I couldn't cook at least that, I'd have starved since my mother came."

I got up and got dressed, and we ate at the table.

It was weird. Really weird. He put water out in glasses. With ice. He made two baked potatoes in the microwave, to have on the side, and then he split them open and poured salsa inside. Both potatoes, his and mine. Like he wasn't going to have butter and sour cream if I wasn't. God knows it's not because he couldn't find any in our house. He even put out paper napkins, folded in half.

It was like what a parent would do. It was like he'd learned to be a parent all of a sudden. Which I guess makes sense when you think about it. I guess that's what you do when you're fresh out of parents.

The venison was like a thin steak with a round bone in the middle, that he'd cooked under the broiler. It was good. Even after all that jerky.

"Thanks for doing all this," I said, but he acted like he didn't hear me.

"I'm sorry to leave you all alone," he said, "but I can't come over tomorrow. I'm going to visit my dad."

I wasn't sure if that was a good thing or a bad thing, and I wasn't sure how to ask.

"Is your mom taking you?"

"No."

"Who's taking you?"

"Nobody. I have to take the bus."

"Oh. Does he know you're coming?"

"No."

"Oh." I chewed about three bites of the steak in silence before I said, "That sounds a little scary."

"I'm not scared of him," he said. "I'm not scared of anything."

"Uh-huh. I see. Well, congratulations on your new status as an alien from outer space. Come on, Will. Everybody's scared of something."

"I know. I used to be. Back when I still cared about stuff. Back when I thought there was still something to lose. Now I don't feel much of anything."

I said, "I don't think that's the good news."

He said, "I don't think so, either."

Then we finished the rest of our meal in silence.

January 8th

Yesterday Will didn't call or come by, which I didn't think too much about. I mean, he said he wouldn't. He said he was going to visit his father. But I didn't think it would take the whole day or anything. So I half expected him to call and tell me how it went. I looked for him online all evening, and I tried calling a couple of times, but it was just this big, weird vacuum.

Then, when he didn't come over today, and he didn't answer the phone, I started to get weirded out.

Sometime around one o'clock I got dressed and put on my new jacket and got all ready to walk over to his house and see if he was around. I even put a pen and paper in my pocket so I could leave a note on his door.

But the minute I opened the door to walk out of the house, I saw Rusty sitting on the curb across the street. I quick closed and locked the door and just stood there, try-ing to get my breath back.

I looked out the window, and he waved at me.

I'm not really sure why I was so surprised. He's sus-pended, and the major focus of his life right now is me and his ultimate revenge. But somehow I still thought of it as a school thing. Inside school, there's this whole ugly world. Outside school, it's not supposed to exist anymore. Unless they follow you when you go get a sundae. But even that. I mean, it wasn't home. Home. Can't there be one single place left that's safe? And then, when there isn't anymore, what do you do?

A minute later he rapped on the door. I put the chain on, just to be safe.

"I guess you know I'd like a word with you, Fat Boy," he yelled through the door.

Then he walked away. But how far away? I couldn't really be sure.

About an hour later I called Uncle Max. Got his ma-chine, which was, like, totally depressing. But then he called me back about twenty minutes later. When I heard the phone ring, I jumped and thought maybe it was Will. But if Will was still AWOL, at least I had someone to talk to about it.

"What's up, favorite nephew?" he asked.

I opened my mouth, thinking I was about to hem and haw. Thinking I halfway didn't know why I called. It definitely wasn't because there was this goon waiting outside my house to kill me. There was nothing Uncle Max could do about that. I either had to call the police—which would be just another reason for him to kill me later—or stay inside, or go out and face it. See how bad it would really be. So I was still sorting it out in my head, why I'd even called him. But when I opened my mouth, it just came out loud and clear.

"I'm worried about Will."

"I see. You think he might try suicide again?"

"No. I don't think so. It's different now. He's getting mad. It's like it's more about other people now."

"Meaning what?"

"Meaning he might try to hurt somebody, but I don't think it'll be himself."

Silence for a moment. I knew I'd said something pretty serious. I knew he was chewing it over. I could picture him holding the phone, chewing on what I'd just told him.

"That's a pretty serious situation for you to be in, Ernie. What do you plan to do to prevent that?"

"I don't know. That's why I'm asking your advice."

"May I assume you have not asked your mother's advice?"

"I can't. Seriously. I mean, this time I really can't. Because she doesn't care about Will. She only cares about me. She'd just be thinking about keeping me safe. So she'd forbid me to ever see Will again. Which would totally make everything worse."

"Do you think Will might ever try to hurt *you?*"

"No. No way. Absolutely not. It's these guys at school. These five guys. Who've been giving us a hard time. My mom doesn't know Will. She thinks he's just nothing but trouble. Everybody does. Except me. And maybe you. I'm thinking maybe you know Will enough to know he's an okay guy. Even though he's having a really hard time right now."

More silence. More chewing over stuff. Then he said, "Unfortunately, even okay guys can do a lot of damage if they're under enough pressure."

"How do I help him?"

"Well, you don't," he said. And my heart kind of fell. "You really can't help anybody else. I mean, unless they want you to. You've been a good friend to him, which is all you can do. But apparently that's not enough. You either have to talk him out of hurting anybody or you have to turn him in. Make sure he never gets the chance."

"But I can't turn him in yet, because I might be wrong. It might be just talk."

"Yeah, but you'd better be careful about the possibility that you might be right. You can try talking to him first, but you're holding a tiger by the tail, Ernie, because think how you'll feel if it turns out you waited too long. If something happens and it turns out you didn't do enough soon enough."

"No. I'll talk to him right away. I will."

"Where is Will right now?"

"Well, I'm not sure. That's part of the problem."

"Don't be too slow to call for help, Ernie. Promise me."

"I called *you*, didn't I?"

"You know, your mother would call the police right now if she heard all this. But I'm trusting you. I'm trusting you'll do it at the right time. Don't let me down, Ernie."

I promised I wouldn't. The last thing I'd ever want is to let Uncle Max down.

The whole rest of today I tried to find Will without leaving the house. I looked for him online every ten minutes or so, and I e-mailed him, and I kept calling his house, but I never got an answer. No Will's mother, no Will.

I was terrified that when my mom got home, Rusty would still be there. Maybe he would say something to her. Or even harass her or something. But she came in at the usual time and smiled at me like everything was fine.

She brought two large double-cheese, double-pepperoni pizzas, and we each polished off one.

"You must be feeling better," she said. "You got your appetite back."

"Right," I said. "Much better."

I'd been so worried about Rusty and about Will that I completely forgot I was supposed to have the stomach flu.

"Guess you'll be going back to school tomorrow."

"Probably so," I said.

Without knowing where Will is. With Rusty waiting outside my door. With no excuse for walking out without my good new jacket. With a clear death threat hanging over my head.

I'm writing this in the middle of the night. I can't seem to get to sleep. Maybe it was that whole pepperoni pizza. But I doubt it.

January 9th

First thing this morning, there was Will. Standing at my door. Like his whereabouts hadn't been unknown for two days. Like he hadn't just scared the living crap out of me.

I invited him into my room while my mom got ready for work.

"How did it go?" I asked.

He looked at me like I was speaking some foreign language. "How did what go?"

"The visit. You went to see your dad."

I thought I saw something flit through his eyes, but his face stayed calm. Like a mask. Like a carved mask. Like it looked after Lisa Muller called him a loser loud

enough for everybody to hear. "Not worth talking about,"
he said.

"I just got worried because—"

"Drop it," he said. "Talk about something else."

"Um. Okay. Did you see Rusty outside?"

"No. Why would I see Rusty outside?"

"Yesterday he was outside all day. That's why I couldn't
come over and see if you were home."

"Well, don't worry," he said. "I've got my pepper spray."

I heard my mom open the front door. I heard her call to
me to have a nice day at school. When I heard her car start
up in the driveway, I sat Will down on the end of my bed
for that serious talk.

"You have to promise me nobody will get hurt," I said.

"Does that count pepper spray in the eyes?"

"No, I mean hurt, like . . ."

"Look, I know what you're thinking. But it's talk, okay?
It's just talk. You stress too much. Don't worry about it."

"Promise?"

"Yeah. Come on. Bring your old jacket. We're going."

I broke the big rule on the way to school. I kept looking
over my shoulder. I couldn't find enough excuses to casu-
ally look around. And I kept thinking I felt them back
there, just about to slam into my back. Like when you're
walking blindfolded, or with your eyes closed. If you think
about a low-hanging tree branch, you just have to stop, or

open your eyes. You keep feeling like it's right there, right about to smack you.

But it wasn't. There was nothing there.

After school we went back to Will's house and got my jacket. And he walked me home. It was raining, a gray, drizzly kind of rain. Just enough to make you feel miserable if you have to walk in it.

We were coming around the corner from his street onto the main drag. I didn't even have to look over my shoulder. We just turned the corner and there they were. All five of them.

Just as I was wondering how confident he felt about taking on five guys with nothing but pepper spray, Will said, "Ernie, run!"

And we both took off, back down his street.

But I only ran about thirty steps before I started slowing down. See, people don't get it. I just can't do what they can do. Like if I went up to Will and put a hundred-pound backpack on his back and then yelled, Run! He'd look at me like, You're kidding, right?

Then again, at a time like that, what else do you do?

I could hear their sneakers pounding on the pavement behind me. Getting closer and closer. And breathing was getting harder and harder. And I had a stitch in my side.

Will looked back and saw I was dropping behind. He

ran back and got me and hauled me along by the arm, which didn't help as much as you would think. He looked behind us and then down to his house, and we both knew we would never make it. And it was all my fault. I was going to get us both killed.

Will made a sharp right and pulled us down the driveway of a total stranger's house. We cut through the backyard. But I'm not sure how good an idea that was, because at the back of the yard was a chain-link fence. And to me that spelled a big dead end. But Will just kept pulling us toward it. I had no idea why. When we hit the fence, Will scrambled over it like it was hardly even there. He stopped and looked back at me, and we both knew how over it was. It's like he didn't get it until just that second. That five-foot fence might just as well have been a sixty-foot greased brick wall with razor wire on top. For me, anyway.

That's when they caught me.

It all happened fast from this point on.

I ended up on the ground, but I'm not even sure how. And while I was rolling around on the ground, trying to get up, I felt the jacket go. It just got pulled right off me. There was nothing I could do. The ground was wet and muddy, and my jeans and shirt were getting soaked through, and it was cold. Without my jacket it was cold.

Then I heard Will yell out loud, really howl, and I knew somebody had hurt him bad.

That's when we got the good news. A grown-up voice. It said, "Hey! What the hell are you boys doing?"

All five jocks jumped over the fence and ran.

I sat up and looked around.

First I saw the five jocks running through the backyard on the other side of the fence. One of them had my jacket in his hand, flapping out behind him, and I could see the whole side of it had gotten soaked in the mud.

Then I turned and saw a woman running out the back door of the house, headed in our direction. Will was sitting on the grass with his hands over his eyes. I thought he was crying. I thought he was just so upset that he was sitting in the mud, sobbing.

Then I saw the little canister of pepper spray lying by his right leg, and I realized what must've happened. He must've tried to use it on one of the jocks. And gotten it turned around on him.

"You boys okay?"

The woman was helping me up. My hip was hurt from falling, but I was trying to convince her I was okay. I didn't want more trouble. I just wanted to get to Will's house and be safe. She tried to help Will up, but he couldn't do it. He just sat there, huddled over, like all he could think about was the pain. Every couple of seconds a little noise would come out of him. It hurt to even watch.

"You want me to call the police? Report this?"

That got Will to his feet. "No, that's okay," he said.

"Thanks, though. I just live down the street. We'll just go home now. We're fine. We just need to go home."

I had to lead Will all the way home. He still couldn't hold his eyes open. He still couldn't see.

I stood in Will's bathroom with him, watching him lean into the sink and run water from the tap into his eyes. At least, for a split second or two at a time. When he could bring himself to open them.

"I'll have to rat them out," I said.

"They'll kill you."

"But I have to get it back. I can't just let them keep the jacket. I can't. I have to get it back before my mom notices it's gone."

"What if they've already ruined it? What if you get to school Monday and find it lying in little shreds in front of your locker?"

"Please don't say that. It makes me sick to think about that."

"Well, we have to think what to do."

"There's nothing to think about. I have to go to school Monday and tell the principal. She might even call the cops. They might have to look in those guys' houses. They're probably too smart to bring it to school."

"You're taking your life into your hands."

"There's nothing else I can do."

He didn't say anything more then. Just turned off the tap. I helped him find his way to the couch, and then I brought him some ice from the freezer, wrapped in a dish towel. He pressed it onto his eyes with a little noise. One of those noises it hurts to listen to. We just sat there awhile, not saying anything.

Then Will said, "I let you down."

"Stop it, Will."

"I did."

"There were five of them. What were you supposed to do?"

"I told you I'd take care of things. And I totally blew it."

I had no idea what to say.

The only thing that could be worse than losing my jacket was if Will took it on as one more thing he'd done wrong. Another terrible thing that was all Will's fault.

Just as I opened my mouth to try to talk him out of it, he said, "Could you go home now? No offense, but I just need to be alone right now."

"Okay, but I just—"

He didn't even let me finish. "Please? Don't talk now. Just let me think about this by myself."

I walked out and left him like that.

Nothing happened on the way home. They got what they wanted. They were done. They must've had enough victory for one day, even for them.

I'm writing this at bedtime. I got home before my mom. If she leaves for work before I leave for school Monday, she won't notice I'm not wearing my jacket. But that's just one day. That's just Monday. After that I don't know.

Monday morning, and Will didn't come pick me up for school. I wasn't sure whether to panic or not. I mean, after all, he only started picking me up at my house to protect the jacket. And the jacket was gone.

Then again, I should have heard something from him. Right? All weekend? I called. I messaged. I e-mailed. But it's like Will didn't exist. Like I might've just made him up.

I sat in my room, chewing my nails and the inside of my lip. Every now and then I'd press my fingers real lightly on my hip, just to feel how sore it was. Like I'd been doing all weekend. I think when other people fall, it doesn't hurt them so much. I guess it's just bruised. I just keep praying it's something that'll get better all on its own.

I knew I had to go to school on my own. But I couldn't leave until my mom left for work. Otherwise she'd notice the jacket was missing.

Then I heard her get into the shower, and I knew this was my chance. My big window of opportunity. On my way past the bathroom I yelled, "Bye, Mom. I'm going to school."

I think she heard me. I heard her say something. But I don't know what it was. I didn't stop to listen. I just got out as fast as I could.

Will was in his room when I got there. He didn't even answer the door. I had to let myself in. His mom wasn't around, either. His mom was never around. The only time I ever saw her was that night at the hospital. And I just sort of saw her hurry by. She never actually said anything to me. I wondered if she'd gone back to L.A. and left Will on his own. If she had, he wouldn't have said anything anyway.

Will was standing in front of the mirror, looking at himself. Just standing there for the longest time. It was weird. He looked different. He was too calm. And he was wearing really baggy jeans. Nothing like he'd ever worn before. Like he took them from his father's closet and made them fit with a tight belt.

I sat on the edge of his bed and watched him watch himself.

"What are you doing here?" he said.

"That's a strange question. We always walk to school together."

"Not today."

He just stood there some more. He turned sideways to the mirror and looked at himself that way, too.

I looked down at the rug by his bed, and something caught my eye. A hacksaw and some shiny metal shavings. Like he'd been sawing through metal, right there in his room. No newspapers, no drop cloth, just right on the carpet. Next to that was a thin metal tube. Well, narrow, I mean. It was made out of thick metal. I picked it up. You could tell which end had been sawed. The other end was smooth, and it had a smooth bump of metal sticking up right at the end. A little bump, like . . . It took me a second to think what it reminded me of.

I looked up to see him looking at me.

That's when it hit me. Like the barrel of a gun. I looked across the room, and there was his father's gun rack. Broken into, moved up from the basement. The two deer rifles were still there. But the shotgun was missing.

The whole thing got so clear and so real that the world backed off and started feeling like a dream. I could feel my heart pound, and everything else was far off. Like the world switched to black-and-white and static.

"Don't follow me," he said. "Think up a reason you're late. Make it a good one, so they know you weren't in on this. Give me at least an hour. Don't be anywhere near the school for an hour."

"You promised, Will."

"This is the best thing for everybody. Believe me." He patted me on the shoulder before he walked out.

Maybe I should have stopped him. Tackled him or something. Sat on him until he listened to reason. But I didn't think he ever would. And besides, I was afraid of him. I was too scared to try to stop him myself. It had gone too far for that. It was beyond my control now. Everybody's control.

I grabbed for the phone.

Dialed 911.

This time I was smart. I told them the exact nature of the emergency. Right away. I said, "There's a boy named Will Manson, and he goes to the high school, and he's on his way there now, and he has a sawed-off shotgun hidden in his jeans. And if you don't get somebody down there to stop him, five people are going to die. I don't know if he strapped it to his leg or what, but he's wearing baggy jeans, and this is not a joke. He's serious. He's really going to do this thing."

"Did you see the gun?" she asked. "How do you know he's going to do this?"

"I'm his best friend," I said.

Then I started to cry, and I hung up the phone.

I ran almost all the way to school. Kind of walking-running, walking-running. As fast as I could make myself go. I don't know what to write about what I was thinking. Because, really, I don't know if I was thinking anything at all. It's like a switch in my brain was turned off. I just put all my energy into going fast.

Well, that's not entirely true. I did have one thought. I thought about what Uncle Max said, about how I would feel if I didn't do enough soon enough. But it was a kind of numb thought. I don't know how else to describe it. It hit my brain and felt cold, like ice, and then I couldn't really feel myself have the thought anymore. I kept it away by saying it wouldn't be like that. It wouldn't. It just couldn't.

When I got there, I saw two police cars and a crowd of kids. It's like nobody was going in. They were just standing there in this big, wide half circle. Nobody was saying a word, which was alien-planet weird all in itself.

I had to push my way through to the front, but it wasn't easy. Usually I'm not good at that stuff. Usually I would stand there and say, Excuse me, or some lame thing like that. But this was not any other day. I just elbowed my way through. I remember being really aware of the sounds people made. Like a grunt, because I pushed somebody. Or a noise that wasn't even a word, but you could sort of tell it meant,

How rude. The only real word was, "Hey." I just kept pushing. My eyes were telling me the crowd was only about ten or a dozen kids deep, but it seemed like I just kept pushing. It seemed to go too slow. It felt like one of those dreams where the monster is after you but your feet are just so heavy. You feel like molasses, creeping along. Just when you want to go fastest, it stops working.

Just before I pushed through the front row, I heard it again in my head. Uncle Max's voice saying, ". . . if it turns out you didn't do enough soon enough . . ."

Will was lying facedown, flat out on the concrete sidewalk in front of the school, his legs all splayed out in those weirdly baggy jeans. Two of the policemen had their guns drawn and pointed at him, even though he was down on his face and his hands were cuffed behind his back.

All these thoughts came into my head at once.

I wondered how they knew which one was Will Manson. I wondered if they called ahead to the principal and made her stand outside or look out the window and tell them which one he was.

Then I thought he looked really powerless, flat out on the ground like that. Handcuffed. And I thought how powerless was so exactly the opposite of what he wanted. I thought how he finally decided to take things into his own hands, and now he didn't even have his own hands. I mean, he had them, but he couldn't use them. So he might as well not have them at all.

Then I realized I was the one who took his power away. Me. His very best friend. I betrayed him. Not that I really had any choice. But still. I betrayed my best friend.

I know it sounds weird, because it was all in just that one or two seconds before he looked up at me. So it's a lot of thinking to do in just a second or two. But it's like all the thoughts came in flashes. They were just there, like on a screen in my brain, until something else flashed in and pushed it away. I don't know how to explain it any better than that.

I saw the shotgun lying a few feet away, all at an angle, like someone had kicked it out of the way.

I saw two of the cops take Will by his cuffed arms and pull him to his feet.

He looked up at me.

This was one of the weirdest, most awful moments of my entire life to date. He looked right into my eyes, and I could see it hit him. I mean, it had to be me who turned him in. There was never anybody else it could have been. But I think he hadn't really stopped to think about what happened until he looked into my eyes. He didn't show a lot of what he was feeling, but you could see it anyway. You could see it change him. He kept a lot of it to himself, but part of it was there on his face.

They marched him by, right in front of me, and he never once took his eyes away from my eyes. I wanted to look away, but I didn't. I couldn't.

It's a terrible thing to say, but standing outside myself like that, I saw him the way he really was. It's like I wasn't in my actual life or the real world, so he looked like a stranger to me. Partway. Halfway. Almost not like my best friend. So I saw him more the way a stranger would. The acne scars on his jaws, and the fresh red-and-white bumps. He had one on his nose, which is always the worst place. And the way his ears stuck out, one a little more than the other. And the way his hair went wild, like somebody had turned a big wind on it. Just for a second I thought I could see how it felt to not be able to look past all that outside stuff. Then I guess I blinked or something, and he was mostly my best friend Will again.

Just as they marched him by in front of where I was standing, he said, "All you had to do was keep your mouth shut. One hour. They'd be gone. All five of them. All your problems would be over. You didn't even have to do anything. Just do nothing, and all your problems would be over."

He wasn't yelling at me. Really not raising his voice at all. But there was something about the way he said it. Something that let me see how big that dangerous thing in him had gotten.

Then I wondered why it took me so long to see.

One of the cops kind of jogged his arm, half turned him away from me, like to tell him to stop talking. Which he did.

But as soon as he could turn back to me, he met my eyes again. This time I didn't feel like I wanted to look away. You know why not? Because I wasn't ashamed. Because I didn't do anything wrong.

They put him in the back of the squad car, the way you see in the movies and on TV. With one hand on his head. Ducking his head down so he wouldn't hit it when they pushed him in. They slammed the door, and he just sat there in the back, looking at me through the window.

Then I did feel bad about one thing. I felt like maybe I could have helped him more. I was his only friend. Maybe if I hadn't pretended he wasn't losing it. Maybe if I hadn't pretended it would never come to this. Maybe there would've been something I could've done.

They drove him away. I watched the car until it disappeared. I watched the street where it disappeared for a while longer. Then I couldn't stare anymore, so I kind of broke my trance and moved again.

That's when I saw I'd been standing right next to Lisa Muller the whole time. And I didn't even know it.

She opened her mouth to say something to me. But it seemed to take a long time. I think the world was moving a lot slower by then. I had time to think that she was going to say something hateful to me, and also that I really didn't care. When you've just sent your only friend off to jail, all that other stuff is small. Nobody can make you feel much of anything else for a while.

What she said was, "Would I be dead?"

I didn't quite get it. My brain was in a funny gear. I said, "Huh?"

"If you hadn't told on him, would I be dead right now?"

Then I got it.

"Oh," I said. "No."

I turned to walk away. I thought I would just go home. I wanted to go home. But I only took a couple of steps. Then looked over my shoulder, and she was still standing there staring at me.

I said, "But your boyfriend would be. And all four of his friends."

Then I turned to go home again, but I ran smack into a cop. Two of them were still there.

He said, "Are you the boy who phoned this in?"

I said, "Yes, sir." Kind of quiet.

"I'd like you to come with us and answer some questions."

Can you imagine having a cop say that to you and not feeling scared? But I didn't feel anything. Not by then. I just said, "Am I in trouble?"

"No, you're our hero," he said. "You're just not quite done yet. We just need you to give us a little more help."

I told them everything, and you know what? It felt good.

The cop I talked to was an older guy, maybe fifty or something. Kind of big and pretty heavy in the stomach, which made me like him a lot more. I didn't figure he was looking down on me.

I just sat there for more than an hour and told him everything. Finally, I got to tell somebody what those guys had been putting us through. I figured the more I told the truth, the better off Will would be, because I could make this guy see how much pressure Will had been under. I told him about Will's homelife, too. All about life in the Manson family. Because part of me thought he'd still be judging Will, because I went through all the same stuff and didn't try to hurt anybody. But I *didn't* go through all the same stuff. I had my mom, and Uncle Max. What did Will have?

The thing that felt best was, when I looked into the guy's eyes, I could see that what happened to us was bad. You almost forget that. Or it's like you don't have a right to think it or something. They don't give you the right to object, or think it's a big deal. But then the cop's eyes kind of mirror it back to you, that nobody should have to get hooked on a rusty lure or get tripped near a flight of stairs or have some goon parked outside your house so you're afraid to go out the door. And some part of you thinks, Oh yeah. I used to know that. How did I forget that?

Then, even after I was done telling him everything I could think to tell him about Will, we talked a little more. He just talked to me for a minute, and I could tell he wasn't really being the cop anymore, and I wasn't really being the boy who called 911. Not for that last minute. For that last minute it was just two people.

He gave me credit for being a real person he might want to talk to. That meant something to me.

"Off the record," he said. "Just between you and me. Was there a split second where you considered it?"

"Considered what?" I asked. I didn't get what he was driving at.

"Saying nothing. Letting it happen."

"Oh. No."

"Not even for a split second. Huh."

"Not really, no." In fact, until he said it, I really hadn't considered that it was there to consider. It just never crossed my mind.

"It's just interesting," he said. "You don't meet too many people who save the lives of their worst enemies."

"Oh. Yeah. I see what you mean. That *is* weird, huh? Thanks to me, they live to torture me another day."

"Well, maybe. Maybe not. It'll be interesting to see. I think the big question here would be, if you save the life of your enemy, is he still your enemy?"

But I really didn't know what to say. I didn't know the answer to that. Then again, neither did he. And he's a grown-up.

My mom was waiting to drive me home. I didn't even know they'd called her. It was kind of a shock to see her there. I guess she had to take off work to come get me.

She was pretty quiet until we left the police station. All she said was, "Where's your jacket, honey?"

I said, "Oh. I accidentally left it in my locker at school." There was a weird pause, and then I said, "You know. Because of all the excitement." Then I felt like I'd said too much, because I could tell she really never doubted me in the first place.

It wasn't until we got to the car that she said it. I could feel it and smell it, and see it in there, waiting to get out. But it wasn't until we were sitting in the car, just before she turned the ignition key, that she spit it out.

"I knew that Will Manson was no good."

I lost it. With my own mother. In my whole life I'd never yelled at my mother. But all the stuff that'd been leaning on me for all those months came spilling out. I just couldn't hold it in any longer.

"You have no right to say that!" I yelled. "You don't know. You don't know him. If you knew the half of what he had to go through. And even if I told you, you'd tell me you could go through all that and not do what he did. You want to say that could never happen to you. Because you want to think it never could. But you don't really know. I mean, now—no, nothing could make you lose it like that, nothing ever will. But if you grew up like he did. You can't know what you'd be like. You have no right to judge him. I won't sit here and let you judge him. It's not fair."

Then I just stopped talking, and we listened to this

giant silence. A big rant like that leaves a big space of silence when it finally goes away. We just sat there and listened to it echo around in that little car.

I thought she was going to tell me I didn't know what I was talking about.

"I guess you know more about him than I do," she said. "I'm just glad you didn't get hurt."

"Will would never hurt me."

She started the car and put it in reverse. Started to back out of her parking space.

"I'm proud of you for what you did today," she said.

"Thanks," I said.

Then we didn't talk anymore for the rest of the way home.

January 13ᵗʰ

I went back to school today.

When I walked down the hall for the first time, everybody turned and looked at me. It was partway like what they did with Will after Sam died, and after he tried to kill himself. Only partway not like that, because not really bad. They got quiet, and they looked at me, but it didn't feel bad.

Still, I got to my locker as fast as I could.

I picked up the lock and tried to work my combination. But it wasn't even a combination lock. It was the kind of lock you open with a key. So I figured I must have the wrong locker. I double-checked the numbers, but it was my locker all right. It just wasn't my lock.

For a minute I stood there with this lock in my hand, wondering.

Somebody had cut off my lock. Or broken it off. And done something inside. And then put a new lock on.

Then I noticed something that looked like a note sticking out of one of the vents in my locker. Right at the level of my nose. I pulled it out. It wasn't a note, though. It was an envelope.

Inside was a key.

This is when I got scared.

I started thinking what would be inside there when I opened it. I thought about snakes. Stink bombs. Paint bombs. Real bombs. I almost walked away. But I had to open it sooner or later.

I stuck the key in the lock, and it fit. I turned it, and the lock dropped open. I lifted the latch and then jumped at the sound it made. Even though it made that same sound every day.

I opened the door and jumped out of the way.

Nothing jumped out at me.

When my heart had stopped pounding some, I looked in.

Hanging on a hanger in my locker was my jacket.

It wasn't dirty anymore. The side that had been all dragged in the mud was clean. Really clean. It was on one of those hangers from the dry cleaners. Those wire hangers covered with paper, printed with an ad for the dry cleaners.

I touched it like I didn't believe it was really there.

I put it on.

After a while I locked up my locker again and started down the hall to my first class. And you know, I did feel like something more in that jacket. In fact, I felt like something more than I had been last time I wore it. It's one thing to have my mom give it to me. It's another thing to have the jocks admit I deserve to have it.

It's like I wasn't exactly the fat boy anymore. I still weighed as much. It just didn't matter as much.

Maybe after school I'd try to call that cop back. Because maybe he really would be interested in the answer to the question.

When you save the life of your enemy, he's not your enemy anymore.

Just as we'd suspected.

August 19th

I'm up at Uncle Max's cabin for the summer.

Uncle Max is working on a new book, so he holes up in his study all day, and then in the evening we have a fire and we get to talk.

Today I told him honestly that I haven't written in my journal in months. Not since right around the time Will had to go away.

He said he understood, and that after a very intense period of journaling my own life, it was okay to take a break.

Then, as soon as he said that, I wanted to write again.

I realized that important things have happened, and if I don't write them down soon, they could be forgotten, gone forever. And my life doesn't seem like such an insignificant thing anymore, that I should let some part of it get lost.

So, just the basics, I guess.

Will got sent to a psychiatric hospital instead of a jail, which I guess is good. I'm not sure if it really works this way in the real world, but I keep thinking maybe he'll get some actual help.

He still won't see me. Every week I call his dad and ask if I can go visit now, if Will has said he's willing to see me. Every week his dad says no, give him more time. So, we have time, right? We have our whole lives.

Sooner or later I think he'll be glad I stopped him before he could make that huge mistake. But even if not, well . . . it's like Uncle Max says. It was either the right thing or it wasn't. It's not about Will telling me it was the right thing. It's about me, and just knowing.

I guess that's it.

Oh. Wait. No it's not.

I've lost fifteen pounds.

I feel kind of stupid even saying that. Because it's hardly anything, compared to what I still have left. I'm probably the only one who would even notice it. And besides, who knows if I can even keep it off when I get home? Home is just such a whole different matter.

Here, it's easier. Because we eat fish almost every night. And because I'm always the one climbing over rocks and hauling up and down the stream to catch it.

I never go up to that pool by the waterfall anymore, though. Well, once I went up just to sit by the waterfall and look. And listen.

But I don't fish up there.

I guess because, so far as I know, Moby and some of the other really big ones still live there. I'm not even sure I can explain why I don't want to try to catch him anymore. It's like I admire him for being so strong and so wily. Breaking so many lines and throwing so many hooks. And even for the times he got squarely caught but somehow managed to get the fishermen to respect him enough to put him back.

It always seems to boil down to the issue of respect.